THE INEVITABILITY OF
DUSK SWALLOWING
TWILIGHT

Also by Dean Campbell

Eboné Blue
(Published by Vantage Press)

THE INEVITABILITY OF
DUSK SWALLOWING
TWILIGHT

DEAN CAMPBELL

The Inevitability of Dusk Swallowing Twilight

iUniverse books may be ordered through booksellers or by contacting:

iUniverse LLC
1663 Liberty Drive
Bloomington, IN 47403
www.iuniverse.com
1-800-Authors (1-800-288-4677)

ISBN: 978-1-4917-0700-5 (sc)
ISBN: 978-1-4917-0702-9 (hc)
ISBN: 978-1-4917-0701-2 (e)

Library of Congress Control Number: 2013916854

Printed in the United States of America

iUniverse rev. date: 08/05/2014

To my mother, my biggest fan

1

"*Crépuscule.*"

"*Cray-pistol?*"

"*Crépuscule.*"

"*Crey-piss* . . . Sorry, I can't say it, Cré."

"Stacy, when you say the second syllable, round your lips tightly like you're puckering up to kiss me. Like this . . ."

"Wait, Cré. My lips ain't thin like yours. You know I got the big juicy lips."

"Okay, Ms. Sexy Lips, sound it from the back of your tongue like this: *Crey-poos-kwel.*"

"*Crey-puss-kill?* Oh my God. Don't roll your eyes at me, Cré. It's hard. Come here."

"Get offa me. I don't want any kisses from you, lesbo."

"Oh, Cré, you know you love it."

Stacy was right. The feel of her soft, full lips against my cheek made my heart beat faster. I smiled and took a sip of my drink. We were at an open-air bar on the beach in Negril, waiting for the sun to set.

"That's an ugly name. I'm sorry. No wonder you shortened it to Cré. How could your mom do that to you?"

"My father gave me that name. She just went along with it at the time because she was so in love with him. She still is. Don't know why. But she hates the name as much as I do."

1

"What does it mean?"

"Twilight. Evening twilight."

"Twilight? Like that stupid movie? Why didn't he just call you Twilight? That's still weird, but it sounds better."

"He's Quebecois. They hate English."

"You musta had a rough time in primary school with that name."

"When I was six or seven, this boy in my class wouldn't stop calling me Pus. I punched him in the face and broke his nose. There was so much blood running from his nose I thought he was going to die. I got kicked out of the school."

"You were seven, and they expelled you?"

"Well, I may have been involved in a few other fights. I was an angry kid."

"Girl, with a name like that, I'd be angry too." Stacy sipped her drink and surveyed the bar. "See that blond white guy with the light-blue shorts and the Tennessee Titans T-shirt?"

I pretended to fix my bun while I stole a look. "Yeah?"

"Look at his watch. It looks like an old Rolex. And he seems to be by himself. What you think?"

"He's been glancing at us ever since we sat at the bar. He's wearing a wedding ring."

"It's been almost an hour, and I haven't seen any sign of a wife or anybody else. He's it. Let's give him the look next time he looks this way."

Stacy swiveled her barstool around and pulled her long braids back away from her face. Like me, she was wearing white short shorts and a fitted, pastel T-shirt.

I took another sip of my drink and followed suit. Our backs were now to the bar, and the sun was about to touch the edge of the sea.

It took one smile to lure our man over to us, drink in hand.

"Hi, ladies. I'm D Ray from Tennessee. Where are you from?"

"I'm Stacy, and this is Cré. We're from Kingston."

D Ray looked me over. "Your name is Cray like cray-cray-crazy?"

"Just Cré," I replied.

Stacy giggled.

"So, just Cré, you don't look Jamaican," D Ray said.

"Oh yeah? And what's a Jamaican supposed to look like?"

Stacy's eyes widened.

"You know. Nice hair, pretty skin, like Stacy here."

"What's wrong with my hair and skin?"

Stacy looked away and shook her head as she struggled to contain her amusement.

"Nothin. Um, I'm just sayin that you have blonde hair and blue eyes like me, and your skin is just as white as mine."

"What you drinking, D Ray from Tennessee?" Stacy interjected, warding off my response.

"Rum and Coke."

"Bartender! Two more Bailey's and a rum and Coke. Sit with us, handsome." Stacy directed D Ray to the empty barstool beside her. "Are you in Jamaica alone?"

"No. I'm on spring break with some a ma buddies, but they took a trip over to Cuba. I couldn't go cuz I left ma driver's license at school, and if I use ma passport, I'd get in trouble when I get back home."

"Aw. So you're all alone? Don't worry. Me and Cré will keep you company. When are your friends coming back?"

"Tomorrow evening."

"You can hang with us if you want," Stacy said as the bartender delivered our drinks.

"Guys, let's not miss the rest of the sunset," I said.

"OMG, Cré. You've seen the sunset in Negril so many times, and every time you get so excited like it's the first time you're seeing it. What's up with that?"

"I don't know. My mom said I was born just after sunset, and my dad said I was the most beautiful thing he'd ever seen."

"Yeah, and then he gave you that ugly name," Stacy said.

3

"I'm with you, Cré," D Ray said. "I saw it for the first time yesterday, and it was the most beautiful thing I'd ever seen. And it's just as beautiful now."

I smiled at D Ray, and all three of us, along with the rest of the bar, cheered the sun as it disappeared below the horizon.

We continued our conversation and finished our drinks in the fading twilight, and at the end of dusk, we ventured out into the night together.

I'm running again from a dark, raging, faceless monster that's bearing down on me with the inevitability of dusk swallowing twilight. My mother is running ahead of me across the sands of an endless beach into the light of the setting sun. She seems not to be aware that I'm behind her and about to be consumed by the monster.

I call out to her, but she seems not to hear me. I lunge forward and try to grab her straight, long, light-brown hair streaming behind her, but the strands slip through my fingers like water. I try to run faster to catch up with her, but she's too fast. As the monster closes in on me, my mother fades into a silhouette that disappears under the horizon with the last rays of the sun. I scream for my mother, and as I'm about to be consumed by the dark mass, I hear a voice whispering my name.

"Cré. Cré. Wake up. I have his watch. Let's go," Stacy whispered. She had her hand on my shoulder, gently nudging me awake.

I woke up beside D Ray's naked body, spread-eagled on his stomach next to me on a king-sized bed in his hotel room. The room reeked of a combination of alcohol, suntan lotion, and D Ray's cologne.

I rolled out of bed, sat up, and accidentally kicked an empty champagne bottle lying on the floor. Stacy and I froze, waiting to see if I had awoken D Ray. He moved his head slightly, his disheveled, blond hair obscuring his face, and he grunted something inaudible but remained asleep.

Stacy threw my bra and panties in my face and then proceeded to tie her shoulder-length braids into a ponytail. She caught me staring at her naked body and widened her eyes as she mouthed, "Hurry up!" Her curvy body and smooth, dark skin looked as beautiful as ever in the dim night light of the hotel room.

I quickly put on my underwear and my shorts and T-shirt before heading out of the room with a fully clothed Stacy. Minutes later, we were strolling on the beach behind the hotel in the direction of Stacy's car, which was parked a mile away.

"You had that nightmare again," Stacy said as she admired D Ray's gold watch before returning it to her purse.

"Was I talking this time?"

"No. But you were tossing and turning. You nearly woke up D Ray from Memphis, Tennessee." Stacy mocked our victim's Southern drawl.

"My mother was in the dream this time."

"It's probably because you're stressing about her not coming to Champs."

"This is the biggest race of my life. I know my mother isn't into sports, but she knows how important to me this is. She should be making every effort to be there for me. She owes me after dragging me all over the world for no reason."

"Calm down, Cré. At least you have a mother."

"Sometimes I wonder if I do."

"Cré Malveaux, that's not nice. No matter how much your mom upset you, she's still your mother. You must cherish that because you never know when you might lose her."

Stacy had lost both her parents at the age of seven. Rumor had it that her parents were drug dealers who got killed by a rival group.

"I'm sorry, Stacy. I—"

"Stop wasting your energy stressing about your mother and focus more on your race. Don't worry. I'll be in the stands giving you all the support you need." Stacy hugged me around the waist as we continued to walk along the moonlit beach. "I'll be there to see you become the national school girls' four-hundred-meter champion."

"I don't know, Stacy. Bridget Shelton is really good."

"Yuh good enough fi beat dat girl. Don't ever doubt yuh self. In fact, let's make sure you're ready to win. If you can beat me to the end of the beach, you're ready. Count to ten, slowly, before you start."

Stacy giggled and sprinted away as I began counting. At five, I was interrupted by an angry voice coming from behind us.

"Hey! Hey!" D Ray shouted as he emerged from the darkness like the monster from my nightmares and sprinted toward me.

3

So here I was, at four o'clock in the morning, one week before Champs, running across a moonlit beach from an angry man screaming obscenities at me and Stacy. I caught up with Stacy in a matter of seconds and then slowed down to her pace, which was not fast enough to outrun D Ray. He seemed determined and surprisingly fast for someone who had been drinking heavily just a few hours earlier. With Stacy running out of breath, and no hopes of outrunning D Ray, I stopped and pulled out my pistol from my handbag. I pointed the chrome-plated twenty-two at the onrushing D Ray.

"Back the fuck up! Wha you want, bway?" I spat.

D Ray slid to a stop ten feet in front of me and fell to his knees. "Please, that's ma daddy's watch," he pleaded in his Southern drawl. "It's been in ma family for five generations. Please, I'm beggin' yew."

"Shut the fuck up!" I barked. The man who just a few hours ago was so macho and virile was now on his knees, stark naked and crying. I couldn't help but notice his shriveled manhood.

"Cré, wat yuh doin?"

I could feel Stacy's uncomfortable stare.

"Gimme your ring," Stacy said to D Ray.

"Ma, ma wedding ring?" he stuttered.

9

"I don't see any other ring on your fingers, bitch," I snapped. I stepped closer to him with menace.

D Ray frantically squeezed off his ring and handed it to Stacy, who dropped it in her purse without looking at it.

While my eyes and the barrel of my gun never deviated from D Ray, Stacy glanced around nervously, hoping that there were no late-night lovers witnessing our crime. She then took D Ray's watch from her purse and threw it at him.

"Thank yew, thank yew, thank yew so much," D Ray gushed. He literally cradled the watch with both hands.

"Shut up," I hissed. "You have ten seconds to disappear."

"God bless yew," D Ray said, incredibly.

"Nine seconds!" I pointed the pistol at him with intent.

D Ray sprinted away, eventually disappearing back into the dark.

Stacy and I ran off the beach and then briskly walked a half mile down the road to where her car was parked.

In the year or so that we'd been picking up tourists in Negril, this was the first time that I had brandished my gun. At the end of each tryst, in the wee hours of the morning, Stacy would steal something valuable from our sleeping stud as a memento, and we would sneak out without incident. I never really understood why stealing something from our lovers was such a big thrill for Stacy, but I went along with the whole thing because it was the only time that she and I made love. At all other times, we were just girlfriends. It was as if we had an unspoken understanding that we could be lovers once a month only in Negril, in the company of an inebriated tourist.

"I'm sorry I almost got you in trouble," Stacy said as we drove to her cottage on a private beach, five miles away from the hotel where we had left D Ray.

"Don't worry about it. Good thing I had the gun."

"Yeah, but what if he had lunged at you and you had to shoot him? Or what if somebody had seen us and called the police? I wouldn't have been able to forgive myself."

"Stacy, you didn't force me to do this with you. I'm not a child. I have a mind of my own. I know you think you're my mother sometimes, but you're not selfish enough." I smiled at Stacy.

"I have to start behaving more responsibly, especially now that I'm going to be running my parents' companies after I graduate."

"Your parents' companies? What companies?"

"The ones that my aunt and uncle run. They were just caretakers until I reached eighteen. Everything is in my name. They've been preparing me for the past two years to take over."

"What about university?" I asked.

"I won't have time, Cré. I'll be too busy. Besides, I don't want to go to university. I don't need to."

Even though we hadn't discussed it before, for some reason, I assumed that Stacy and I would be going to the University of the West Indies together. Her declaration of her decision not to go saddened me. But what concerned me more was her suggestion that our Negril adventures had run their course and had come to an end.

I felt like I was losing her.

4

The pistol exploded and echoed around the stadium like thunder, and I lunged out of the starting blocks. I tried to block out the lightning storm of camera flashes and the roaring crowd while I concentrated on my breathing and my stride. My left hamstring was holding up nicely. A week ago, I had tweaked it while Stacy and I were running from D Ray.

I was running comfortably and, after the first bend, I was in a good position. I approached the second turn in the lead. Bridget, the defending champion, was in second place. If I could hold on to this lead, it would be my biggest victory. I glanced up into the stands hoping that by some miracle I would see my mother there cheering for me. I lost focus and, coming out of the final bend, Bridget took the lead.

I suddenly became aware of the thick humidity, which seemed to be clogging my lungs and constricting my stride. The stadium lights seemed to be shining directly into my eyes. I closed them for a moment and conjured up the faceless monster from my nightmares. I was determined not to get caught by the dark mass bearing down on me, and suddenly my lungs opened up and my legs broke free. I glided past Bridget and thrust my body chest first into the tape.

The stadium monitor confirmed that I, Cré Malveaux, was the new Jamaican high school girls' four-hundred-meter champion.

I exchanged fake kisses and quick hugs with Bridget and the other girls before joining in celebration with my coach and teammates. I waved to the section of the stadium where Stacy and the rest of my schoolmates were screaming for me. I wished my mother was there too to cheer for me. She hadn't even called or sent me a text all day.

My mother was in Canada on one of her business trips. She and I had just started getting along after years of dragging me around the world with her.

Since taking up track and field on my return to Jamaica, I had tried unsuccessfully to get my mother to take some interest in my sport. "Cré, all that running in the sun is gonna make your skin dark and mess up your chances of winning Miss Jamaica," she would say whenever I tried to get her to come to one of my meets. It didn't matter to her that I wasn't interested in becoming a beauty queen.

My mother was first runner-up in the 1989 Miss Jamaica World contest and insisted she lost the crown only because her complexion was darker than the winner's. My mother was a mixture of black, white, and Indian. The girl who won was white. I was the product of an affair between my mother and a blond-haired, blue-eyed Canadian and had inherited my father's features and complexion. My father, a married hotelier from Montreal, met my mother while she was competing in the pageant.

A year after I was born, she moved us to Montreal from Montego Bay to be closer to my father. Less than a year later, the relationship sourced, and she dragged me along on a wandering pursuit of love that took us to Toronto, Vancouver, New York, Miami, Bogota, Barcelona, Paris, and London. I was often upset with her for taking me away from my new friends, but I could never bring myself to complain because she was usually distraught.

But approximately three years ago, while we were living in London shortly after Mother had left her fourth husband, I rebelled. After my second arrest for drug possession, she and I both found out how angry I was. A tearful counseling session followed where she also found out that I was frequently self-medicating with all kinds of drugs and alcohol and was having sex with anyone who would smile at me. She made the decision to make a final move back to Jamaica shortly after that session.

We settled in Kingston, where she met her new husband, David Thompson, an elected official. David sometimes drank too much and occasionally flirted with me, but I determined to tolerate him and do everything I could to make the marriage work. At two years, it was my mother's longest marriage so far.

I fingered the gold medal hanging from my neck while I tried again to call my mother. It was 10:00 p.m., and she hadn't answered any of my calls or returned any of my messages all day. I polished away an imaginary spot on the medal with the sleeve of my tracksuit while I waited for my mother to pick up. Her voicemail service picked up, and I hung up without leaving another message. I had my bare feet up on the dashboard of Stacy's car, a bright-red, late-model, BMW 3 Series sedan.

"She must have a good reason," Stacy assured me as she pulled out of the stadium parking lot. "Maybe she's on a hot date."

"Stacy, that's not funny. I'm really worried about her."

"Oh Cré, your mom is probably out celebrating some big business deal she closed today. You need to stop worrying and do some celebrating of your own. C'mon, you beat the best high school four-hundred-meter runner in the entire country, and you're smart, and you're a hot *gyal*." Stacy smiled and winked at me. Her dark-chocolate complexion made her big, beautiful smile appear impossibly white.

"You know, Cré, sometimes I wish I was you," Stacy continued. "You're tall and beautiful, you're multilingual, you get good grades, and you're a track star. It seems like everything you try you do well at, even shooting. Remember how hesitant you were to try it at first? Then when you did, you hit the bull's-eye with nearly every shot. And last weekend when you pulled out your gun on that guy, you weren't nervous or anything. It was like you had done this before. You scared me, by the way. You had a look in your eye like you would have shot that guy if he had tried anything."

"You really think I'm beautiful?" I interjected.

Stacy sucked her teeth and rolled her eyes. "Bitch, you know all the boys love your long, pretty, blonde hair and blue eyes. You should enter Miss Jamaica like your mom wants."

"You're prettier than I am. Why don't *you* enter?"

"I'm too sexy for Miss Jamaica," Stacy said. "Dem can't handle all a dis sexiness." She leaned forward in her seat and slapped her rear before flashing that smile that often made me swoon. Stacy had a way of easing away my worries, concerns, or bad moods with that smile. She was my comfort and, especially in the last few months with my mother being away so often, had become my emotional means of last resort.

"Stacy, we should stay in tonight instead of going out. We could watch a DVD and go to bed. You're staying over, right?"

"No, Cré. We already planned this. Remember we were going to celebrate the end of track season win or lose. Plus we need to meet some guys, especially now that we're not going to be doing the Negril thing again. We need to settle down. We need boyfriends."

"I don't need a boyfriend. I have you," I responded. I had put one foot across the line.

"I'm serious, Cré. I told you last weekend that I've been thinking about my life and where it's going. I've been doing some stupid things and dragging you along in the process. You could have gotten in trouble *and* you almost got injured because of me. I'm going to be running businesses with a lot of employees and a lot of money at stake. I'm at the stage now where I have to be more responsible and more serious about life. I need . . . We need to be in steady relationships. There's gonna be some nice men at the place I'm taking you to tonight. We'll have boyfriends before the end of the week."

I pulled my foot back across the line. I felt very lonely. I wished my mother was home. I wished I could run to her.

I ran out of the bathroom to get the phone, but it was only a text from Stacy saying that she would be ten minutes late, as usual. It was almost twelve o'clock, and I still had not heard from my mother.

I dropped the phone on the bed and finished drying myself, and then I threw the damp towel on the bed. I rummaged through my underwear drawer and noticed the barrel of the gun I had brandished a week ago sticking out through the black thong I was searching for. I took it out and aimed it at myself in the mirror. Stacy had given me this gun to use at the range, but she encouraged me to take it with me whenever I would be in any of the high-crime areas in the city. I wasn't sure where we were going, but I intended to take it with me just in case.

I was shocked when Stacy first introduced me to her collection of six handguns. And I was more shocked when she informed me that not only were her aunt and uncle aware of her possession of the unlicensed weapons, but they also had given her two of the handguns as presents. Besides the handguns, Stacy's aunt and uncle had given her the cottage on the beach in Negril, where we spent many a weekend, and the BMW she drove before she was old enough to get a driver's license. Stacy also was given the leeway to come and go as she pleased and to stay out as late as she wanted, even on a school night. Her aunt and uncle had become her guardians after both her parents were killed.

I met Stacy at my mother's wedding reception in a private club owned by my current stepfather. She was by herself sitting in a swing in the arboretum behind the club where I had gone to escape the clutches of some of my new stepfather's sleazy colleagues, who were being a little too friendly on the dance floor. I had noticed her dancing closely with my stepfather's younger brother, Tanny. Dressed in a red gown with a yellow hibiscus blooming from her hair, she was the brightest flower in the garden. She beamed a smile at me, and when I smiled back, she exhaled a stream of smoke from a joint she was smoking. She offered me the half-finished joint, but I declined and maintained my distance to avoid the cloud hanging over her head.

She squinted at me through heavy eyes. "I know you. You're on our track team. You're fast for a white girl."

"I'm not white," I snapped. "And would you mind putting that out? I have a meet this week, and they do random testing."

"Have you looked in a mirror lately? If you truly believe you're anything but white, you *need* to get drug tested."

I gave her an evil look and turned to walk away.

"Girl, I'm playin' wit you," she said. She dropped the joint and ground it out with the sole of her yellow heels and then fanned at the haze around her. "Happy?"

I uttered a cold thank-you.

"You're welcome," she said, before melting away my icy defensiveness with her radiant smile.

We began to talk, and eventually I sat beside her. Before long, we were talking as if we had known each other all our lives. She teased me about the little red dress I was wearing and the effect it was having on my stepfather's guests. She playfully plucked the flower from her hair and planted it in mine. We became best friends after that day.

The first place we hung out together was the gun range, where she introduced me to her guns and encouraged me to take up shooting. I was a quick study—I'm not sure why, but I didn't tell her that my Colombian stepfather had taught me to shoot almost ten years ago. Hitting the target felt as easy as pointing in the mirror.

While I was aiming at myself in the mirror, I heard a car pull up the driveway. I looked out my bedroom window and saw my stepfather's car. He was supposed to be in Trinidad and wasn't expected back home until Monday evening. I quickly deposited the gun in my handbag on my bed and again looked out the window. He stumbled up the steps toward the front door. I hoped that he would go straight to bed as he usually did when he came home drunk.

He instead came straight to my bedroom.

"Cré, I need to talk to you," my stepfather slurred as he banged on my door.

"One second!" I shouted. I tightened the belt around my bathrobe before opening the door. "David, is everything okay? I thought you weren't coming back till Monday."

"Well, it's April first, so April Fools!"

He walked in and sat at the end of my bed. He was dressed in the same black suit and white shirt he had been wearing when he left for Trinidad on Friday morning. The only thing missing was the pink tie. His normally short, perfectly combed, and trimmed Afro was knotty and unruly. His eyes were bloodshot and watery, and his dark face was shiny with an oily film of sweat.

"Seriously, why are you back so early?" I folded my arms firmly across my robe.

"I heard that your school came second at Girls Champs. Did you win your races?"

"We didn't make the four-by-four relay final, but I won the four hundred," I replied.

"That's excellent. I'm telling you, you should take that track scholarship from UCLA. I think you have a really good chance of going to the next Olympics."

"I know, David, but I want to go to school here. All my friends are here. UWI has a decent track program. Don't worry. Just make sure that when I qualify for the Olympics, you'll get Mommy to come watch me. By the way, have you heard from her?"

"Your mother shoulda been at the stadium cheering for you this weekend."

"You know Mommy isn't into sports."

"That's no excuse!"

I took a step back, startled by my stepfather's angry response.

"You're more beautiful than your mother, inside and outside," he continued in a more subdued tone.

"Thanks," I muttered with uncertainty. My stepfather's countenance seemed angry and was a far cry from the mischievous mug he usually displayed when flirting with me. I began to sense that my mother had messed up again.

"Do you know why your mother's in Canada? Be honest."

"She told me she was going there on business," I replied. I believed my mother at the time, but now I was afraid to look my stepfather in the eye.

"I really loved your mother. I have never cheated on your mother. Not once."

"David, I'm sorry. Please give Mommy another chance. I don't want our family to break up again. Maybe you and her could see a counselor and try to work things out."

"It's too late, Cré. I'm done with her. But I still want to play a part in your life. You're about to go to university and you'll need help, so I'll be there for you."

He stood up and offered me a hug.

I accepted the hug, and he held me tightly and kissed me on the cheek. His breath reeked of alcohol.

I attempted to end the hug after it became uncomfortably long, but he tightened his grip and attempted to kiss me on the lips. I evaded his lips and tried to pry his thick, sweaty hands from around my waist, but his grip was firm.

"Cré, I can take care of you. I can make you happy. I can make you a woman."

"David, you're drunk. You're not thinking straight." I tried again in vain to pry his arms loose. "Stacy's coming to pick me up in a few minutes," I whimpered.

"I don't care," he growled as he attempted to kiss me again.

I slapped his face, and then he threw me on the bed and pinned me down.

"Do you know who I am? I'm David Thompson, minister of trade and commerce. I run things in Jamaica. Most girls would kill to be with me. You tink because yuh white yuh too good fi mi! You're nothing but trash just like your mother."

I stared horrified into the face of the angry, two-hundred-pound hulk on top of me and saw only the dark, faceless monster from my nightmares.

8

The dark, faceless monster from my nightmares invaded my reality, breathing alcohol fumes and barking obscenities. It shoved me onto my back on my bed and then pounced on top of me, gripping my neck with one tentacle, ripping open my robe with another, and forcing my legs apart with another two. I struggled frantically to free myself from beneath the monster, but it was too strong and too heavy.

To my right, I noticed my gun dribbling out of my handbag. As I reached into my handbag, I felt the monster trying to force another of its tentacles inside me. Determined not to be taken by the monster, I snatched the pistol from the handbag, pointed at the dark, faceless head, and squeezed the trigger again and again until it collapsed on top of me.

I rolled the monster's silent, heavy carcass off me and sprang to my feet, horrified by the sight of blood gushing from the space where its face was supposed to be. My trembling trigger hand, still wrapped tightly around the gun, was soaking red with blood.

I stumbled into the bathroom and was startled by a crimson face framed by red-highlighted hair staring back at me from the mirror above the basin. I dropped the gun in the basin and shed my robe before stepping under the shower and turning the water full blast onto my face. I lathered myself from head to toe and scrubbed frantically, repeating the process over and over until I was convinced that I had gotten rid of every speck of blood from my hair and skin.

I stepped out of the shower and dried myself with a white towel, meticulously checking for any residual specks of blood I may have missed. I wrapped my hair in a towel and tiptoed back into the bedroom, trying to avoid getting any blood on my feet.

The smell of blood, which seemed stuck in my nostrils, became stronger as I reentered the bedroom. The sight of the bloody, mangled face of the corpse of my stepfather lying on my bed shocked me anew. I grabbed a comforter from the closet and threw it over the body, making sure to completely cover the blood-soaked halo around the head.

I had shot to death a man before, years ago in Colombia, when I was a little girl. The man was a stranger who was trying to kill my stepfather, Sebastien, and my mother. I remember my feelings of fear and terror gradually being replaced with a feeling of relief while watching the assassin lying on the floor in front of me, bleeding to death. But that incident could not have prepared me for the bitter cocktail of fear, guilt, and panic that was coursing through my body, knowing that I had killed my mother's husband.

I was startled by my phone ringing. It sounded louder than normal. I could tell by the ringtone that it was Stacy. Instead of picking up the phone, I ran to the living room, the towel on my head falling off along the way, and pressed the buzzer that opened the front gates. I peeped through the curtains eagerly waiting for Stacy's car to pull up to the front entrance.

I watched Stacy get out of her car and trot up the steps toward the front door while tugging down on the short hem of a body-hugging, white, sleeveless dress she was wearing. I opened the front door, dashed out, and hugged her as she got to the top of the stairs.

"Cré! Why yuh naked? Yuh shaking like a leaf. What's going on?"

I said nothing. I couldn't. My knees began to buckle, and I held on tightly to Stacy's neck.

Stacy held me up and eased me back into the house and then closed the front door. She helped me to the closest chair, stooped in front of me, and looked past my nakedness into my terrified, teary eyes. She wiped my tears away with her knuckles and caressed my wet hair.

"It's all right, Cré. It's all right," she whispered. "Tell me what's wrong."

"No police. Put these on," Stacy said. She handed me underwear, the tracksuit I was wearing earlier when I left the stadium, and a black New York Yankees baseball cap.

"But . . ."

"Cré, trust me. That's the last thing you want to do."

"Then what am I supposed to do? They're gonna know that I did it."

"Don't worry about that now. You have to get out of here."

I took the items of clothing from Stacy, and she went back into my bedroom. Just before, she had donned a pair of latex gloves she found in the kitchen and set about disabling the security cameras and erasing the day's recordings. She had also wrapped her shoes with plastic wrap before entering the blood-splattered bedroom to retrieve the gun.

While I dressed, I wondered if the reason why she was being so adamant about not calling the police was the unlicensed gun she had given me.

Stacy returned from the bedroom with the gun heavily wrapped in paper towels and asked for my passport.

"Stacy, I'll tell the police that it's David's gun."

Stacy grabbed me by both shoulders and locked eyes with me. "Cré, I want you to listen to me carefully. Your stepfather was one of the most ruthless dons in Jamaica. Half of the police in Kingston are on his payroll. When his people find out that you killed him, the police can't protect you even if they want to. If you go to the police, you'll be dead in a week. I'm the only chance you have, okay? Where is your passport?"

"Passport? Where am I going? And what about my mom?"

"If you're right that Mr. Thompson caught your mother cheating on him, she might not be safe either. After I get you outta here, give me the address or the name of the hotel where she's staying and I'll have some of my people check in on her. Now, where is your passport?"

"In the computer desk drawer in my bedroom," I replied.

"I'll be right back." Stacy ran back into the bedroom.

My heart began to race, and I felt like I was running out of air. I was horrified at the thought that my mother might be in danger. I tried not to entertain the worst-case scenario, but it crashed into my mind and remained there. I called my mother again and got her voicemail again. I left a frantic message for her to call me or text to let me know she was okay. I also sent a text message pleading for a response.

"Cré, how come you have so many passports?" Stacy shouted from my bedroom. "Jamaican, European, Canadian, and a green card?"

I didn't respond. I was still battling the negative thoughts that had taken up residence in my head. I was desperate to find out if my mother was safe.

Stacy rushed out of my bedroom with the passports and green card. She studied each document for a few seconds, after which she handed me the European passport and told me to put it in my pocket. She returned to the bedroom with the other passports and the green card. Moments later, she returned from the bedroom and grabbed me by the arm. "Let's go. Leave the phone. They can track you with that," she said.

I complied, allowing Stacy to hustle me toward the front door. I waited at the front door as she instructed, while she peered outside. Given the all-clear to come out, I followed her out to the car and lay down in the backseat as directed.

"Don't worry, Cré, I'll take care of you," Stacy said before starting the car and driving off.

I was surprised at how calm and controlled Stacy was. She had taken charge of the situation with the confidence of someone who had absolutely no doubt about what to do. The carefree girl I knew, who seemed not to take school or anything else seriously, was methodical. I hadn't taken her seriously when she was going on and on during the past week about growing up and being more responsible, but now I was seeing her in a different light.

During the drive to her home, Stacy continued to reassure me that everything was going to be okay. Her calmness put me at ease somewhat.

But fear for my mother's well-being dominated my thoughts.

"The driver is here, honey!" Stacy's aunt shouted as she peeped out the window. She tugged at the hem of the immodest little red dress she seemed to be popping out of. She and her husband were on their way to a party when Stacy brought me to their home.

Stacy's uncle came running into the living room. He had removed his jacket, and his shirtsleeves were rolled up. "Exactly 2:30. Right on time, as usual," he said as he looked at his obscenely big, bejeweled watch. He shoved a thin wad of five-hundred-euro notes into my hand. "That's five thousand euros. Put half in your pocket and half in your handbag," he instructed. "If you can't get on the flight to Amsterdam, try to get on a flight to Miami or New York, and try another airline when you get there, okay?" he continued. "And remember: don't talk to the driver. He doesn't know who he's transporting and doesn't want to. He won't leave until you get on the plane and your flight leaves, so if you see him hanging around the airport, just ignore him."

I divided and separated the money as instructed and then hugged Stacy's uncle and aunt. I thanked them and apologized for ruining their evening and then hugged Stacy. I felt safe in Stacy's embrace, and at that moment, I wished there were some way I could stay with her, or she with me. I had a burning hole in my stomach from worrying about my mother, but the prospect of separating indefinitely from my best friend made my heart ache. My whole body was welled up with emotion, but tears refused to come.

"Remember not to text me, or call, or e-mail, or write under any circumstances. And stay off Facebook," Stacy commanded softly. "We'll communicate only through Angie for now, okay. She'll take good care of you. I love you."

Stacy's uncle coaxed me and Stacy apart.

I slid on a pair of designer shades that Stacy had given me and gathered my luggage, which consisted of a Burberry handbag and a small matching Pullman that contained only the tracksuit I wore to her house. I was dressed in a pair of blue jeans and a blue-and-white striped shirt from Stacy's uncle's closet, because they were the only clothes that fit me. I was also wearing the same sneakers I had arrived with, and the Yankees cap, under which my hair was bundled.

I stepped out the side door into the yard where the open door of a heavily tinted black BMW was waiting. I could barely make out any details with the shades on.

I slid my luggage in first with the help of Stacy and then stole one last hug before slinking into the car. The driver, who had remained seated and silent, acknowledged only the sound of the closed door and immediately drove off. I waved good-bye, even though I knew I could not be seen through the dark tinted windows.

"Seatbelt."

I instinctively looked in the rearview mirror to see the face where the order had come from, but it was partially concealed by the low brim of a baseball cap.

I put on my seatbelt and went over the plan in my head. I was to fly to Amsterdam where I would meet Stacy's cousin, Angie, who would arrange to get me new identity papers that I was to use to go to Canada to live. The idea was to have the authorities and my stepfather's people believe that I was hiding out in Europe. But I was more concerned about my mother's well-being and getting to her as quickly as possible.

The driver turned on the radio and Bob Marley's mourning voice filled the cabin of the car. "You runnin' and you runnin' and you runnin' away. But you can't run away from yourself," he wailed over and over.

11

The driver dropped me off at the departure area of the Sangster International Airport in Montego Bay at exactly 4:00 a.m. I walked into the brightly lit airport terminal and was surprised by how crowded it was so early in the morning. I headed directly to one of the automated ticketing booths, which were mostly idle.

US Airways had the earliest flight to Amsterdam, which was scheduled to depart at 6:00 a.m., but only first-class seats were available. I attempted to purchase a ticket, which cost almost twenty-five hundred euros, but a credit card was required. I walked across the hallway, through the ropes, and joined the queue for the US Airways ticketing counter. While I waited on line, I looked around for the driver and was relieved to see the familiar logo of his baseball cap with its low brim covering his eyes. I found myself glancing behind me every so often to see if he was still there.

A few minutes passed before I was called to the counter by a woman who looked a lot like the former four-hundred-meter champion I had beat just hours before.

"Good morning. How can I help you?" the woman recited.

"Hi. I need a ticket for the six o'clock flight to Amsterdam."

"It's full," the woman answered without looking at the monitor.

"Are the first-class seats gone too?"

"First-class tickets on this flight are around two hundred and fifty thousand Jamaican dollars," the woman said, still without checking her computer.

"Book me a first-class ticket. And would you be so kind as to give me the price in euros?" I was trying my best not to sound annoyed.

The woman clicked away at her keyboard. "I need your passport," she said without looking up.

I perched my sunglasses on the brim of my baseball cap, retrieved my passport from my purse, and placed it in the woman's outstretched hand. I also took out the twenty-five hundred euros I had in my purse.

The woman opened up the passport and then looked up at me. "Ms. Malveaux . . ."

"Yes?" I answered nervously. My heart began to pound.

"You beat my little sister yesterday at Champs."

"Uhm, sorry," I stuttered, feeling more relieved than apologetic.

"Oh, don't be sorry. She'll get you back next time." The woman smiled and resumed typing.

I smiled back at the woman and my heart rate subsided.

"How come you're flying to Amsterdam? Don't you have school today?"

My heart picked up speed again. The woman seemed to be staring at me with suspicion. "Uhm, I uhm . . . My grandmother is dying, and I want to see her before she goes." I slipped my sunglasses back over my eyes.

"I'm sorry to hear that."

"Thank you."

"The ticket is 2,479 euros."

I put the twenty-five hundred euros on the counter and quickly removed my hands so that the woman wouldn't notice that I was trembling.

"I hope you get there in time to see your grandmother," she said before handing me my passport, boarding passes, and change.

"Thanks again," I said while I collected my boarding documents and money, desperately fighting to control my trembling hands. The sight of the driver still watching over me did little to calm me.

"Have a safe flight," the woman chirped as I walked away from her counter.

As I headed to the security checkpoint, I tried not to think about the desperate situation I was in. I thought about my mother and the many airports she had dragged me through during my childhood. We always seemed to be running to catch a flight.

I walked out of the customs area of Schiphol Airport at 6:59 a.m. local time. It was the end of a twenty-hour journey that took me from Montego Bay to Miami, Newark, London, and finally, Amsterdam. My trip was smooth except for having to endure a "random" search at Heathrow. Initially, I thought I was being arrested.

I scurried toward the pick-up area, hoping that the Dutch police weren't outside waiting for me. As soon as I passed through the sliding doors, a cold headwind, which I was insufficiently dressed for, smacked me in the face. I stopped and looked around, hoping to see Stacy's cousin. A tall white man in a black leather jacket and dark glasses approached me and addressed me by name. I was sure this time that I was caught, so I answered him with resignation. He led me to a waiting car where I was relieved to see a woman fitting Stacy's description of her cousin.

"Angie?" I half-asked and half-declared.

"Yeah man, no doubt," she replied coolly from the backseat.

"I thought it was the police," I muttered. "That was my second scare today."

"Why? Them search you a Heathrow?"

"Yes! I thought . . ."

"Them always searchin' people that fly from Jamaica." Angie had a wry smile.

I felt immediately at ease with Angie, who had the same confident demeanor as Stacy, if not the same sense of style. I couldn't help but stare at her red fauxhawk, the tattoos crawling up her neck, and the multiple piercings on her face and ears.

"So I heard you won the four-hundred at Champs. Congrats. That's a hard race. I used to run the hundred meters, but I wasn't fast enough."

I wanted to ask Angie if she had received any news from Stacy about my mother, but I couldn't get a word in. For the entire twenty-minute drive, she reminisced about her days as an average high school athlete.

The driver dropped us off in front of a row of anonymous, semidetached houses.

Angie led me to the gate of one of the houses before stopping. "The cops found Thompson's body a couple hours ago, so it won't be too long before they find out that you're in Amsterdam."

"What about my mom? Did you hear anything?"

"No. Not yet. They took Stacy out of school to ask her some questions, so she didn't get a chance to find out about that yet. But we'll find out something soon."

"Is Stacy going to be in trouble?"

"No, man. Don't worry. She can take care of herself." Angie patted my arm reassuringly. "All right, there are two people inside who are going to help you. Don't ask them any questions. And don't talk to them unless they ask you a question, okay?"

I nodded and followed Angie into the basement apartment.

We were met by a smiling, middle-aged, Chinese couple who were both smoking cigarettes. There were no introductions. The couple immediately extinguished their cigarettes and directed us through the smoke-filled living room to another room in the back of the apartment.

On one side of the back room were two basins and two hairdryers separated by a table covered with hair products. On the opposite side of the room was a camera on a tripod and a desk with a laptop connected by cable to a printer. The Chinese woman directed me to sit at one of the basins while the man sat in front of his laptop.

Angie promised to return in two hours and left without saying anything else to either me or the couple.

"Beautiful," the Chinese woman said. She swiveled me around to face the mirror and beamed a yellow smile at her creation.

I didn't recognize myself. What was left of my hair was a short, spiky, bleached-blonde tuft, and I was heavily made up with extra emphasis on eyeliner and eye shadow. Before I could react, I was whisked over to another chair to have my picture taken.

The woman handed me a white blouse to put on. I changed and sat down in front of the camera. She came over and fiddled with my hair, asked me to smile, and then retreated.

I conjured up a smile for the camera.

"Perfect," the Chinese man declared before returning to his laptop.

The woman took me to another room where several items of expensive-looking clothes and accessories were laid out. Within minutes, I was decked out in black six-inch-heeled boots, faded designer blue jeans, a turquoise turtleneck sweater, and a long, tan spring coat. I was also given a new handbag and a suitcase with additional clothing.

I followed the woman back into the front room where Angie was waiting. At five feet, ten inches, I was already taller than everyone, but now my heels made me tower over them.

"Wow, these guys are good," Angie said. "You look totally different."

"It's ready," the Chinese man interjected, handing Angie my new passport.

While Angie studied the passport, I looked at my new image again in the mirror and was still shocked by the stark difference from how I used to look.

"Wha you think?" Angie said as she handed me the passport.

I studied the passport. My new name was Janet Jones, and I turned twenty-three on February 29. My real birthday, my eighteenth, was April 7, just a few days away.

"This passport is good for only seventy-two hours, and it's only good for travel between Paris and Toronto. So if for any reason you can't make it to Toronto within that time, don't use it, and take it to the Paris drop-off spot. Don't forget to drop it off immediately after you leave the airport. You remember the drop-off spots, right?"

"Yeah, man. Don't worry. Everything cool," Angie said.

She gave the Chinese man a pat on the shoulder and her phone chirped. "That's our ride. You guys are the best." She gave the man a stack of one-hundred-euro notes, which he handed to his companion.

I exchanged smiles with my anonymous helpers and followed Angie out the door with my new set of luggage in tow. A cab was idling in front of the house.

Angie glanced at her watch. "You should be in Paris by 3:00. As soon as you get there, take the earliest flight to Toronto. How much money you have left?"

"About twenty-five hundred euros," I answered.

"Here's another five thousand." Angie handed me an envelope. "The drop-off location for the passport is in there and the address of the hotel you should book into once you get to Toronto. Also the name you should book under. Someone will contact you at the hotel."

I put the envelope in my new purse, and Angie rapped on the roof of the cab. The cabdriver came out and put my luggage in the trunk.

Before I went into the cab, Angie held my arm and looked in my eyes. I knew in that instant that my worst fears had been realized. I listened numbly while she told me that the bodies of my mother and father were found in a car not far from my father's house in Westmount, Montreal. They had both been shot execution style.

I couldn't feel or hear anything after that, and the cab ride to Schiphol and subsequent train ride to De Gaulle seemed to run by in a nightmarish haze.

14

Raindrops trickled down my hotel room window like tears, distorting my view of the CN Tower, which looked like a twisted needle protruding from the Toronto skyline. Down below, a colorful traffic of vehicles, people, and umbrellas flowed through the arteries of the city. I could feel tension coursing through my veins, pounding in my wrist where my watch was tightly strapped on. I looked at the time as I loosened the watchband. It was 8:30 a.m., half an hour before I was to be picked up to meet the person who was going to give me a new life.

I had arrived in Toronto overnight and booked into the hotel right after dropping off the passport. Immediately upon entering the hotel room, I turned on the television, hoping to hear that somehow Angie was misinformed and my mother was alive.

The sliver of hope that I allowed myself to feel was crushed when the newscaster announced the killing of my parents. It was being reported that the Canadian police believed that my stepfather killed my parents in a jealous rage when he found out they were having an affair. It was also being reported that that the Canadian police believed there to be a connection between the murders of my parents and the death of my stepfather, and that I was being sought by the Jamaican police. The good news was that I was believed to be hiding out somewhere in Europe.

When they showed pictures of my father, mother, and stepfather, I found myself staring at my father's picture with hatred. I blamed him for not allowing my mother to get over him and move on with her life. I hardly knew my father, whom I spoke to once a year when he called to wish me happy birthday and whom I last saw when he visited Paris while my mother and I were living there. That was the first time I had seen him since my mother and I left Montreal when I was about two years old. He had gentle, pale-blue eyes and appeared too old for my mother. I remembered wondering at the time if his wife and children knew about us and if they knew that he was in Paris ruining my mother's marriage. I was upset and hardly spoke to him or my mother while he was there. Now I wished that I had spoken up and let them know how I felt.

I glanced at my watch again and went to the bathroom to take another look in the mirror to assure myself that I had sufficiently recaptured the new look I was given. I disliked my heavily made-up look, but it was a necessary disguise, plus it covered up the bags under my eyes that had developed from crying myself to sleep. I looked over my outfit and then grabbed my luggage and headed downstairs to the checkout counter.

When my ride arrived, the doorman took my bags and led me outside where the driver was waiting by the open trunk of a black, heavily tinted Audi S8.

"Good morning, Ms. Steele." The driver greeted me with a professional smile and opened the door for me. He was tall and handsome, with shiny black hair and dark eyes.

"Morning. Thank you," I replied. I wondered if I was going to be stuck with this latest moniker. After I got into the car, I noticed that he tipped the doorman.

"Thanks for tipping the doorman. I have a lot on my mind. How much was it?" I reached in my purse and pulled out a ten-euro note.

"Don't worry about it." He smiled at me in the rearview mirror.

"No. Take it." I thrust the folded note over his shoulder.

He held my hand. "Hold on to it. Just buy me a drink sometime," he said.

I met his eyes in the rearview mirror and quickly pulled my hand away. His touch made my heart speed up and my skin burn. "Okay. I guess I owe you one, uhm . . ."

"My name is Nadim," he responded. "We'll be running into each other often, so you'll get the opportunity to buy me that drink. You should put your seatbelt on."

During the twenty-minute ride, I learned from Nadim that I was to be the new personal assistant to his boss, Yasmine, whom he described as a "businesswoman." I was driven to a large estate in Mississauga, a leafy suburb outside of Toronto. At the entrance of the grounds, the car was closely watched by a pair of rotating security cameras on either side of a wide metal gate. Midway up the long, gravelly driveway, the car was intercepted and then chased by a pair of bounding Doberman pinschers.

"You're not scared of dogs, are you?" Nadim asked.

"Only the ones that bite," I replied.

"They bite only ugly people, so you're safe," Nadim said, glancing up at the rearview mirror in anticipation of a smile that didn't materialize.

He stopped in front of the main house and quickly got out to open my door. He introduced me to the dogs and then left me at their mercy to get my luggage from the trunk. The dogs sniffed me and then escorted Nadim and me to the front door where a tall, strapping, middle-aged, black woman with a short, gray Afro was waiting.

"Miss Yasmine want you to take her to her office right away," she said to Nadim in a Jamaican accent. She shooed the dogs back outside and commandeered my luggage from Nadim.

"That's Maxine. She's usually much friendlier," Nadim said as he winked. He then walked me through the first floor of the cavernous mansion toward Yasmine's office. After a few twists and turns, we arrived at the office, which was open.

Yasmine was engaged in an animated conversation on the phone. She waved us in and mouthed a thank-you to Nadim, who took his cue to leave. She indicated to me to sit in one of the chairs facing her desk while she wrapped up her phone conversation. She was dressed in running gear, and her jet-black hair was in a ponytail. She appeared to be either in her late thirties or early forties. A prominent sign on her desk indicated that her name was Yasmine Khan, and her framed bachelor's and MBA degrees on the wall behind her reaffirmed it.

At the end of the phone call, she stood up and extended her hand. "Sorry to keep you waiting, Ms. Steele," she said.

"No problem, Ms. Khan," I responded as I sprung out of my seat and accepted her hand. I was sure now that "Jackie Steele" was going to be my new permanent name.

Yasmine had a strong grip for someone so thin. She was at least as tall as me and had olive skin like Nadim's. She had big, dark-brown, almond-shaped eyes framed by perfectly sculpted eyebrows. She looked me over while I sat back down.

"What size shoes do you wear?" she asked.

"Ten," I answered tentatively.

"Good. We wear the same size. There's some running gear in the bathroom. We're going for a run." She pointed to a door on the right-hand side of her office and picked up her phone.

I headed to the bathroom wondering if I was about to be recruited as a personal trainer. I washed the makeup off my face, changed, and returned with the old clothes and shoes in hand.

Yasmine instructed me to leave my clothes in the bathroom and then led me out of her office and onto the grounds, where we were immediately met by the dogs. She initiated a comfortably paced jog, and the dogs ran ahead of us.

"I'm sorry about your parents," Yasmine said.

"Thank you," I replied.

Yasmine engaged me in small talk about running while leading me on a slow jog down a path that took us to the outer edges of the estate. Once there, she picked up speed in what seemed like an undeclared challenge. The path, which continued along the border of the property, narrowed and was filled with steep inclines and declines, and it wound around trees with hanging limbs that forced us to duck.

After fifteen minutes of trying to avoid decapitation, the challenge ended where it had begun with Yasmine victorious. The dogs, which had tracked us all the way, gathered around me as if trying to console me.

During the walk back to the house, Yasmine described herself as a business associate of Stacy, an assertion that would have left me bemused had it been made before my life turned upside down and Stacy financed and orchestrated my elaborate escape.

Yasmine surprised me by how much she knew about me and how readily she revealed intimate details about her own life. She even knew about the incident in Colombia years ago when I shot to death a man who was trying to kill my then stepfather and my mother. Yasmine delighted in the fact that I killed my current stepfather before he could rape me, and she went on to relate in painful detail how she was raped by a gang of mujahideen from Afghanistan who had taken refuge in her village in Pakistan. She was only thirteen at the time and had gone to fetch water. She related with a steely defiance how she used one of the rapists' own machine guns to kill them while they were sleeping. She sought to assuage any guilt I was harboring for killing my stepfather by detailing to me how she killed her own father after he brutally beat her mother, who was trying to stop him from bringing Yasmine before the tribal elders to stand trial for indecency. He had accused Yasmine of shaming him after she told him she was raped. Her mother tried to save her from certain death by taking her through mountainous terrain in the middle of winter to a Canadian-run refugee camp in Afghanistan. Her mother collapsed and died less than a hundred meters from the camp.

The fact that Yasmine trusted me enough to be so open with me on our first encounter made an impression on me. I felt some perverse comfort in the fact that her story was worse than mine, but more importantly, I was seduced by this seemingly blind trust she had placed in me. My body, mind, and soul relaxed, and at that point, I had developed a trust in her that was automatic and wholehearted.

Perhaps that is why, when she revealed to me the nature of her business and what my new job was to be, I felt little apprehension. Officially, I was being employed as her personal assistant, but I was to be much more. The tasks of fetching coffee and running errands were nonchalantly lumped together with providing personal security and protecting her business interests.

"This job will give you the chance to enhance your athletic abilities, expand your language skills, and fine-tune your ability to shoot straight," she said with a straight face. "You're a survivor like me, and we can help each other negotiate what is a very tough world out there," she continued.

I hadn't expected to be recruited as a trained killer, but I didn't bat an eye when she detailed the six months of specialized training I was to receive. In truth, I felt like I could not turn down Yasmine's offer, not because I was afraid of her or of what would happen to me if I ended up on my own but because I felt a kinship with her. I had an obligation, it seemed, to help my fellow survivor, my sister, continue to stay alive in what was indeed a dangerous world. So I looked past any apprehension I felt and ran in the opposite direction of where my moral compass was pointing. In my mind, at that moment, there was nothing more moral than helping my family—my new family—survive.

I was shipped off to training the evening of my birthday just two days after arriving at Yasmine's estate. Earlier that day, after I had gone on a run with Yasmine, played with the dogs, and had breakfast with Nadim and the perpetually grumpy maid, Yasmine handed me my new passport in between a phone conversation and dismissed me from her office with an unceremonious wave of her fingers.

It was just two weeks prior that I was making plans with my mother and Stacy for my eighteenth birthday celebration. Now my birthday was passing by without fanfare or acknowledgement. I attempted to check Stacy's Facebook page to see if she still had my birthday party invitation posted, but she apparently had closed her account.

I started to believe that my life as Crépuscule Malveaux, born on April 7, 1993, was over. I had died and was now Jackie Steele with a Canadian passport that said I was born on August 5, 1989. I wondered if this is how my mother felt each time she married a new husband and took his name.

17

I was flown to a small town in the northern part of the Yukon Territory, where I was picked up by my trainer, a steely-eyed Russian Amazon with a graying, blonde crew cut. She introduced herself as "Dick" and referred to me as "Pussy." I smiled and waited for her to smile back. But she instead got in my face and glared into my eyes with raging eyes.

"If you want to leave Yukon alive, if you don't want to get fucked, move smile off your face now." Her breath smelled of cigarettes.

"I'm sorry. I thought you were joking." My smile had vanished the moment her face closed in on mine and our eyes locked.

"You think this is joke? You think you're here to train for clown?" Her face was still no more than a half inch from my face, and her eyes were unblinking.

I felt like a small dog cornered by a bigger dog. I averted my eyes, turned my face away from hers, and bowed my head. I could feel her hot breath on my ear.

"Get in the truck, Pussy."

I approached the passenger side of her old, beat-up pickup truck.

"Nyet! In the back."

I was incredulous but dared not show it. I avoided further eye contact, dropped my luggage in the back, and climbed in.

She slammed the door after getting into the truck and sped off.

Even though I was dressed for winter, and it was the middle of spring, I was freezing. It was fifteen minutes of torture until she stopped at a gate that seemed like an entrance to nowhere.

"I hear that you like to run," she said after she got out of the truck.

I didn't respond.

"You see cabin over there? We run to cabin." She pulled a knapsack from the cab of the pickup and threw it at me. "You carry my bag," she said. Then she walked to the gate, opened it, and started jogging along the snow-covered pathway toward the cabin, which looked like a tiny speck in the distance.

I grabbed her knapsack, which felt heavier than my duffel bag, and ran behind her. Halfway to the cabin, I had slowed down considerably as my chest began to burn and my heart felt like it was going to explode. When my torturer-in-chief noticed that I was lagging behind, she sprinted toward me and spat abuse in my ear until we reached the cabin. At the end of my run, I was more concerned about my hearing than the health of my heart.

Aside from toughening me up and training me in the dark arts of murder and mayhem, my trainer spent the next three months trying to drain me of all empathy. Each day, I would have to maim a caribou and then cut its throat until she felt that I had no more apprehensions about killing.

"Don't see eyes, don't see face, see only target," she barked at me when I hesitated in shooting a caribou cow that was suckling its calf.

Seeing the frightened calf looking around, confused as if trying to decide whether to run or stay by its fallen mother's side, sickened me and made me realize that Cré Malveaux was very much alive and was no assassin.

Later that night, while cocooned in a sleeping bag on the floor of the creaking log cabin I shared with my taskmaster, I decided to confine Cré and her abundance of empathy to the basement of my mind so that Jackie Steele could emerge and be the heartless killer she was meant to be. As the training progressed, I learned to keep the two apart. I left the Yukon not only physically prepared for my new career but also mentally prepared for my new life.

I returned to a Toronto that seemed a different place from what it had appeared to be three months prior, perhaps because I left during spring showers and returned in the middle of a blazing summer. I stripped down to my T-shirt, exposing my newly enhanced biceps. Nadim didn't recognize me when I approached him in the airport arrivals waiting area, and even after I removed my trucker cap and oversized shades, he hesitated before saying my name like he was asking a question. My hair had grown considerably and I wasn't wearing the heavy makeup he was used to seeing on me.

"Ms. Steele, you're even more beautiful than I remember," he gushed.

I insisted that he call me Jackie.

We stopped at a bar on the way back, and I bought him the drink he'd suggested on the day we first met. Nadim was curious, peppering me with questions about my past and background in between his flirting. I was evasive and mostly unresponsive to his flirting, not because I was shy or concerned about revealing my true identity but because I had become Jackie Steele, a deadly, tightly wound muscle who knew nothing other than how to kill. But by the third drink, Cré emerged from her hiding place. I began to respond to his flirting if not his inquisitiveness. I was smiling again, if only for a brief time.

The very next day after I returned, Yasmine ordered me to cut and dye my hair back to the short, bleached-blonde look captured in my passport, and she gave me my first assignment. I was told to make a statement, which meant a public and messy assassination. No reason, explanation, or justification was given and none was expected. I returned Cré to the basement, and Jackie executed the assignment without nervousness or apprehension.

But when the night came, I could not sleep. Images of the target's faceless, eyeless head exploding haunted me.

That was the first night that Yasmine came to my bed. I received her attentions willingly and came to depend on it particularly after a kill.

18

Who I was at any given time depended on who I was around or what I was doing. I was Jackie when I was around Yasmine or when I was carrying out her orders. I was usually Cré around Nadim, Maxine, and the dogs. I got along well with the easy-going driver, the fussy maid, and the playful Doberman pinschers, but my relationship with Yasmine was more complex. Most of the time, she was undoubtedly my boss, but after each killing, each maiming, each bombing, each arson, she came to my bedroom and offered herself to me as my equal.

We were equals to the extent that she allowed me to be as aggressive with her as she was with me in bed. It was understood that our time in bed was more about release than passion, more symbiosis than love. After we each were satisfied, she would immediately leave for her own bed without saying a word, and I would roll over and fall asleep, content in the knowledge that no dark, faceless monster would haunt my dreams.

Most of my free time was spent in the company of Nadim, usually in the guest cottage where he lived, watching track and field or watching a Jamaican news magazine program, hoping for an improbable glimpse of Stacy. I had developed a friendship with Nadim that filled some of the empty space in my heart and my life caused by my separation from Stacy. Nadim and I often flirted with each other, but neither of us dared cross the undeclared but very real line that separated us.

Yasmine was aware of the friendship between Nadim and me, and not once did she ever express concern or display jealousy. So it was a big surprise when she burst in on us one evening while we were watching the World Track and Field Championships. I thought initially that it was because I was screaming too loudly while watching the girl I had beaten to win my gold medal at Girls' Champs barely missing out on a World Championship gold medal.

"I need you right now," she snapped as she immediately walked back out without even acknowledging Nadim.

Nadim and I exchanged bemused looks before I scurried after Yasmine. While running to catch up with her, I checked my phone and realized that she had called me.

"Yasmine, I'm sorry I missed your call. I was so caught up with—"

"Shut up," she hissed without breaking her angry stride back to the main house. Her bathrobe was flapping in her wake and her bed slippers were slapping loudly against the bottom of her heels.

I followed a step behind her, in silence, as she led me to my bedroom.

"Get in!" She slammed the door shut after I stepped inside and slapped my face when I turned to face her.

A part of me wanted to hit her back and another part of me wanted to cry. I didn't know who to be. I searched her big, dark-brown eyes for an explanation and, perhaps, for whom I should be.

"I could've been in danger," she seethed. Her eyes betrayed a vulnerability I had never seen in the almost two years since I began working for her.

I understood then that the real source of her anger was jealousy. That realization made me feel special and powerful, and I grabbed her head with both my hands and kissed her.

Her response was passionate and eager, unlike the controlled, dutiful attentions I was used to getting from her. She shared with me what I wished I could have shared with Stacy, and for the first time since we began sleeping together, I gave her Cré.

Yasmine giving herself to me without me having killed, maimed, or blown up something felt like a step forward in our relationship. But when she left me in bed afterward without saying a word, the same as always, I felt emptier and lonelier than usual. Unable to sleep, I fantasized what it would feel like cuddled up in bed with Stacy, but each time I drifted off, the dark monster of my past reared its faceless head and woke me.

After countless failed attempts to get past the monster, I jumped out of bed and ran to Nadim's cottage. I let myself in to find him up, sitting in the same chair where I had left him only hours before, staring at me as if he had been expecting me. We had a brief, wordless conversation before he got up and hugged me. He led me to bed, lay beside me, and spooned me. His smell, his breathing, his heartbeat, and his warmth harmonized into the perfect lullaby, and I fell asleep with no monster in sight. After that night, each time Yasmine abandoned me, I sought refuge in Nadim's bed.

This continued for three months, until Yasmine's inevitable reaction.

Yasmine had assigned me to execute a couple, a job I completed with cold professionalism, only to realize at the end that a little boy had been present and witnessed the entire incident. In the two years I had been Yasmine's henchwoman, I had never been assigned a job where a child might have been present. The little boy stared at me and said nothing. I slowly backed away from him as if he were a predator about to pounce, and I ran off into the night.

That night I couldn't sleep. The boy's stare haunted me. I kept having flashbacks to when I killed my first caribou while it was suckling its calf. I couldn't wait for Yasmine to come in and go through the motions so I could run to the comfort of Nadim's embrace. But she never showed up. At midnight, I went to her bedroom, but she wasn't there. I walked to Nadim's cottage, but he wasn't in either. I went back to my room and sat out the night, stuck between speculations about Yasmine and Nadim, and the little boy's stare.

Early the following morning, Yasmine summoned me to her office.

"I hope you slept well," she said, staring into my tired eyes. A sense of satisfaction seemed to be beaming from her eyes. "Come with me," she ordered.

She led me outside where Nadim was standing by an open car door. He looked tired too.

We drove in silence for a half hour before arriving at a farmhouse that seemed abandoned. The rundown farmhouse contrasted with the bright autumn leaves of the surrounding forest.

I was nervous getting out of the car, and all I could think about was protecting Nadim. I glanced back at him as Yasmine led me into the old farmhouse. My body and mind were tense in anticipation of what I was certain was going to be some sort of ambush.

Instead, there was a man tied to a chair with a hood over his head. Yasmine removed the hood and ripped the tape off his mouth. She circled the man until his squinting eyes adjusted to the light.

"So, I hear you're pretty handy with a switchblade," Yasmine said.

"Untie me and give me a blade, and I'll show you," the man snarled at Yasmine in what sounded like a Boston accent.

Yasmine produced two switchblades from her coat pocket and tossed one at the man's feet. "Untie him," she ordered as she removed her coat and sweater.

I untied the man, but he stayed in his chair and looked at me suspiciously.

"She's not armed. Your only chance to leave here alive is that blade," Yasmine said to the man. She turned her back on him and walked five steps away. She nonchalantly flipped open the switchblade and turned around to face him.

Even though it seemed apparent that Yasmine and this man were about to fight each other, I couldn't discount the possibility that both of them may be in collusion and might attack me or that the victor, whichever it might be, would then attack me. I began to slowly back away from both of them.

The man picked up the switchblade and began circling Yasmine, who stood still and stared ahead, her blade dangling from her limp hand.

My heart leapt into my mouth when the man lunged at Yasmine from behind.

Yasmine evaded the man's attack and slashed his arm in one motion. The man ignored the cut. As the blood dribbled down his arm, he went after her again with the same outcome. He was quick, but she was quicker. She was balletic in her movement and ruthless with the blade. Each time she evaded and slashed her prey, she looked me directly in the eyes. I went from fearing for her back to fearing her.

The man, bloodied and weakened, eventually collapsed to his knees, his blade sliding out of his limp hand.

"I'm sorry, Ms. Khan. Please have mercy," the man pleaded feebly.

"You stole from me, you made your own deals, and you bragged about it. And didn't you say you were going to teach me a good lesson? Hmm? Weren't you going to slash my face and give me a good ass-fucking? Well, here's your mercy."

Yasmine pulled the man's head back by his red Mohawk and stared at me for an eternal moment before slitting his throat.

"No one does things behind my back or defies me and gets away with it," she hissed over the sound of the man gurgling to his death.

Before the man's killing, my mind had been racing at full speed, trying to figure out if Yasmine intended to kill me or Nadim or both of us. But now I relaxed in the realization that she just wanted to remind me that she was undoubtedly in charge and what she was capable of. She had laid out an ultimatum that I would have to heed if I was going to survive.

The cleaners arrived while we were on our way back to the car. The three-man crew ran by as if we weren't there and went straight to work. During the drive back, I found myself constantly glancing up at the rearview mirror, perhaps trying to discern what state of mind Nadim was in. His eyes seemed less tired and more alert than before, but they did not betray any fear. Both Nadim and I remained quiet while Yasmine loudly conducted business on her cell phone.

When we arrived back at her estate, Yasmine had me accompany her to her office.

"I don't usually do field work, but every now and then, I have to get my hands dirty to keep sharp," Yasmine said, her big, dark-brown eyes sternly focused on my tired eyes. "As you know, there's no free lunch around here. So since I did your job today, I want you to make up for it by assisting Maxine for the rest of the day."

She dismissed me by turning her back to me and making a phone call.

I took my cue and went straight to the kitchen, where Maxine was chopping up goat meat. "Yasmine wants me to work with you today," I said.

"You look like shit. Wha wrong wid you?"

"I didn't sleep last night. I couldn't—"

"Yuh mus' go to yuh bed a night an' stop run roun' wid Nadim. Yuh can start wid di bathroom dem. De cleaning supplies inna di broom closet. Time yuh do some real work roun' here instead a deh strut roun' di place like yuh a model."

Maxine typically had a very direct way of expressing herself, but I was not prepared for this level of brusqueness.

My half-closed eyes opened wide and my eyebrows arched up more in surprise than anger.

"A who yuh a stare down? Yuh tink mi 'fraid a yuh? Beg yuh gwaan go clean de bathroom dem before tings get rough up inside ya." Maxine had one hand akimbo and the other gesticulating at me with the meat cleaver.

I imagined the cleaver stuck between her eyes.

I was ordered to clean all thirteen bathrooms in Yasmine's sprawling estate, including the one in the maid's quarters, Maxine's residence. Maxine inspected each bathroom, making sure every faucet was sparkling and no spot was in sight. I was made to reclean anywhere a spot was found, visible by me or not, and I seemed to have missed a lot of spots. Particularly in the toilets. She made sure to admonish me loudly in front of whatever staff was around at the time.

By the time my humiliation was complete and my work was deemed acceptable by Maxine, it was 8:00 p.m. I had now not slept in thirty-six hours. I had a cup of tea and went straight to my bedroom. I spent the next four hours thinking about what to do to diffuse the situation. At the forefront of my thoughts was making sure that Nadim was not killed.

At midnight, I went to Yasmine's bedroom and knocked on the door.

"Come in, Jackie," she said.

I entered and found her in bed reading a book, her glasses perched on the bridge of her nose. She was wearing a white tank top and white briefs, and her long legs and arms seemed to be glowing. Her hair was tied up into a bun atop her head, exposing her long neck.

"Can I talk to you for a second?" I asked sheepishly.

"Sure. What's up?" she said with a sigh. She closed a black book with bright blue letters that read "Eboné Blue" and laid it on the nightstand. She removed her glasses and placed them on the book. She then folded her arms and looked up at me in stern anticipation.

"I just want you to know that I'm not sleeping with Nadim."

"Don't you think I already know that? Do you think you and Nadim would still be alive if I thought that? You're so naïve. I'm amazed each time you come back from an assignment in one piece because you can be so stupid sometimes. I know you're not sleeping with him, but the security guards don't. The landscapers don't. The maids don't. Maxine doesn't. Don't you think they know that I'm fucking you? What kind of impression of me do you think they have if they think you're two-timing me with Nadim? You know the kind of business I'm in, and surely, you must know that my success and my very well-being are dependent on maintaining the respect of everyone around me. Listen, I know you two are in love with each other—"

"No, we're not."

"Yes, you are. I see the way you guys both light up when you're around each other. I also see that you're both trying to suppress it, which is a good thing and the main reason you're both alive. You're doing the right thing. You can't allow yourself to succumb to love in this kind of business. It's dangerous, trust me.

"I've already spoken to Nadim. You are not allowed to hang out with him here or anywhere else, and needless to say, you will no longer be sleeping over at his cottage. Now come to bed and get some sleep. You look like the walking dead."

Yasmine was right. I did have feelings for Nadim that I was trying to hold back, not because I was worried about what she might do but because I was still hanging on to the hope that one day I would see Stacy again and she would love me back.

I crawled into the bed with Yasmine with a less heavy heart than when I had entered her bedroom, relieved that I didn't have to execute my plan B, which would be to take Nadim and run. I collapsed onto my back and she stripped my pajama bottom off. Then she buried her face between my legs. I pretended it was Stacy's strong hands forcing my legs apart and Stacy's steady tongue caressing me to ecstasy.

All the tension of the past forty-eight hours gushed out of me, and eventually I floated off to sleep.

I woke up in Yasmine's bed to find her standing over me, her dark face fuming like storm clouds. Her shiny, black hair was styled in a tight bun that pulled her sculpted eyebrows into severe, angry arches. She was wearing a black blouse underneath a dark-gray business pants suit and stood in black heels. She had a manila envelope in her left hand and an iPad hanging from her right hand, which she was steadily slapping against her thigh.

"What time is it?" I croaked as I sat up and stretched.

"It's almost midday," she replied before throwing the iPad into my lap.

On the tablet was a remarkably accurate artist's sketch of me under the newspaper headline "Woman Sought in Execution-Style Killing of Seven-Year-Old's Parents."

"*You left a witness behind?*" Yasmine's scream made me jump.

"I was adhering to your own 'Don't hurt kids' policy," I mumbled.

Yasmine flung the envelope to the floor and lunged at me, punching me in the eye, and then she grabbed me by the neck and started slapping my face. I was too surprised to retaliate. I used one hand to protect my face and the other in a futile effort to pry her fingers from around my neck.

After the flurry of slaps and punches ended, Yasmine got off me and held her head with both hands as if trying to stop it from exploding.

"I swear you're going to be the downfall of me," she said in an accent that had changed to South Asian from Canadian. "You're so fucking stupid," she continued. "Wouldn't common sense tell you that it doesn't apply when it comes to witnesses? I swear, if it wasn't for Stacy . . . You have forty-eight hours to fix this!" She picked up the envelope and threw it at me. "Get outta my sight!" she spat.

I walked out of Yasmine's bedroom with the envelope in hand and only my pajama top on.

The envelope contained the location where the child was being held in protective custody. That she acquired the location so quickly reinforced my belief that she had members of the police force on her payroll. I couldn't help but think that she might be sending me into a trap despite her suggestion that Stacy was still protecting me. Regardless of Yasmine's intentions, I had no plans to carry out her latest order. As monstrous as I had become, I could not bring myself to kill a child.

I passed Maxine on my way to my room. She looked at me with disgust and shook her head. I don't know if she knew why Yasmine was mad at me, and I didn't care. All I could think about was how I was going to escape Yasmine and avoid getting killed—or arrested. As far as I was concerned, I had less than twenty-four hours to disappear, hopefully with Nadim. Somehow, I knew this day was coming, so I already had cash, identities, escape routes, and alternate destinations in place.

By nightfall, I had already briefed Yasmine on how I was going to get past the police and silence the witness. She was much calmer than she'd been earlier, and she made a point to warn me not to kill any cops. She also surprised me by apologizing for giving me a black eye. She advised me that, unlike on previous assignments where Nadim would drop me off and pick me up at a predetermined rendezvous point, I would be leaving the estate in the trunk of the Audi. After completing my assignment, I was to immediately go to the plastic surgeon who was going to change my identity. I was going to be away for at least six months while I recovered from the surgery and my new identity papers were being prepared. She also made me know in no uncertain terms that all the costs would be coming out of my future remuneration.

At ten o'clock, I climbed into the trunk of the car with my gear. I waited for the car to pull out of the estate, and five minutes later I pulled out my phone. I called Nadim and asked him to stop the car and let me out.

"I can't," he replied. "We're being followed."

I was not surprised that we were being followed, but I was worried that it might be the police. My plans would have to change if they were indeed the police. The display on my phone dimmed and the trunk got dark again.

"Hello? Jackie? You still there?"

"Yes, Nadim. I was just thinking. Pop the trunk. I'm going to try to see who's following us. What kind of car is it?"

"It's a gray Chevy Malibu. It's in the right lane behind a red Mini Cooper."

I opened the trunk just wide enough for my binoculars to peep through. I instantly recognized one of the men who had removed the body of the man Yasmine slashed to death a couple of days ago. I was relieved it wasn't the police.

"It's Yasmine's people. Nadim, I need to talk to you about something."

"You know why Yasmine is having us followed?"

"Yes, but don't worry about that right now. I need to ask you something."

"Okay, shoot."

"Do you love me?"

"What?"

"Okay, that was unfair. You don't have to answer that. Look, I'm leaving and I want you to come with me. I know this is sudden, but I made my decision today. I like you and I think you like me too, so before I disappeared, I wanted to at least give you the option of coming. I have several safe escape routes and enough money to start a new life."

As I waited for what felt like an eternity for his response, I realized how nervous I was. My heart was pounding harder and louder than it had on my first kill.

"Why are you leaving? What happened?"

"Nadim, I know you know what I do for Yasmine, but despite all the terrible things I've done, I can't bring myself to kill children. I don't like the life I'm living, and I want to reset and start over, hopefully with you."

"Whose children does she want you to kill?"

"A kid who witnessed a killing."

"Is that the child in the paper who's been put under police protection?"

"Nadim, the less you know the better. Are you coming with me or not?"

"Okay. I'll come with you. What's the plan?"

Although I was desperate for Nadim to come with me, I was surprised that it was so easy to convince him. I instructed him to change lanes and speed up. As soon as I got a clear sight of the car following us, I shot out the left front tire and the car veered out of control. It crashed into the car to its left.

"Find the closest parking garage and go there. Use the GPS."

Within fifteen minutes, we were parked in an underground parking garage in Toronto, after which Nadim let me out of the trunk. I hugged Nadim briefly before breaking into and jump-starting a Ford Focus parked on the same level. I took off my turtleneck, put on a black wig, and then gave Nadim a baseball cap to wear.

"So where are we headed?" Nadim asked me.

"Colombia. By the way, my real name is Crépuscule. Crépuscule Malveaux. But you can call me Cré."

Nadim and I drove all night and most of the following day to Halifax, stopping only for gas. I told him my story during the drive, but for most of the journey, we took turns behind the wheel while the other slept.

We arrived in Halifax around 5:00 p.m., approximately eighteen hours after leaving Toronto. We ditched the car and checked into a motel, after which I set out to find a boat that would take us to Colombia on very short notice. After two hours of searching, I finally found someone who was willing to leave that night. The owner of the boat turned out to be a man I had met at a bar in Toronto six months prior. I was having a drink while waiting for Nadim to pick me up after a job I had completed earlier than planned. He was a drunken charmer who proposed to me and offered to sail me around the world.

Captain Bermuda Jack, as he called himself, agreed to take Nadim and me to Colombia for the price of only twenty thousand Canadian dollars. It was about a quarter of the money I had saved over the two years I worked for Yasmine. I had lied to Nadim about having enough money to start over, but I was hoping that my former stepfather would help us. I hadn't seen or heard from him after my mother divorced him about ten years ago, and based on his high-risk profession as a drug-dealer, I couldn't be sure that he was alive. But he was my only hope.

Captain Jack was a tanned, leather-skinned Bermudan whose face seemed permanently flushed as if he were perpetually drunk. He was clean-shaven with a slick, gray ponytail, and he had a pair of small silver earrings glistening from his ears. He had a constant glint in his green eyes as if he knew something that you didn't.

We left the marina around midnight and sailed for a day and a half before stopping for fuel in Baltimore.

During our first night together, Nadim didn't attempt to make love to me, which I assumed was because of the close quarters on the boat and the proximity of Captain Jack.

"No matter what happens, just remember that I love you and I have your back," Nadim said, before we curled up in bed and fell asleep in each other's arms.

The following day, he seemed quiet and detached.

"I have a bad feeling about your boyfriend," Captain Jack whispered to me on one of the occasions Nadim disappeared inside to get out of the sun.

"We're going through some big changes and he's stressed," I responded.

"Did he give you that black eye you're hiding behind those shades? I can throw him overboard if you want."

I laughed. "He wouldn't be on this boat if he did."

We docked at a Baltimore marina around midday. About ten minutes into our stop, we were surrounded by the police who seemed to appear from nowhere. All three of us were taken into custody, and before I knew it, I was sitting in front of two men who identified themselves as "Homeland Security agents." One of the men proceeded to relate to me my life story to date, the source of which had to be Yasmine or Nadim. Since it seemed unlikely that these men were on Yasmine's payroll, I concluded that Nadim must have panicked and betrayed me.

The men read charges against me, but they threatened me with extradition to either Jamaica or Canada to face justice. I sensed that they wanted more than just my prosecution.

"So what do you want from me?" I asked.

"We want Yasmine Kahn."

Even though I felt that Yasmine probably had a price on my head by now, I couldn't even think of ratting her out. In my mind, she was still a kindred spirit trying like me to survive. I couldn't possibly betray her.

"I can't help you," I replied.

The two men then abruptly left the brig without saying anything further.

During my time alone in the interrogation room, I felt like the gray walls were closing in on me. I didn't want to go to jail, and in that moment, I felt like death would be preferable to incarceration. I wondered how the police found out I was on Bermuda Jack's boat. If Captain Jack recognized me as the assassin whose sketched likeness was all over the news, why did he not give me up in Canada? Why wait until we got to the United States? Nothing was making sense to me. I felt guilty about getting Nadim in trouble.

In the midst of my feelings of guilt and worry, the door opened and Nadim strolled in. He stopped across from me. He looked neither worried nor frightened.

I noticed a badge dangling from his neck, and my stomach contracted into a painful knot that felt like someone had kicked me in the gut. I could feel hot tears beginning to stream down my cheeks.

"Cré, I—"

"Don't! You have no right to call me by that name!"

"Ms. Malveaux, if I didn't bring you in, you would have been dead in two weeks. Yasmine has people everywhere, and she's more ruthless than you can imagine. I brought you in to protect you. I meant it when I said I would always have your back."

I avoided eye contact with Nadim and ignored his assertions that he had my best interests at heart. I was still trying to absorb the fact that the man I placed my complete trust in, whom I had hoped to help me get over Stacy, was a cop. I felt stupid. I couldn't help but think that Yasmine was right—I *was* naïve.

"Your best bet is to cooperate with the agency. If you testify against Ms. Kahn, this is what we can do for you: you'll have complete immunity from all the crimes you committed under her direction, and . . ." Nadim paused for a moment before continuing. "And we can help you with your case in Jamaica."

The second part of Nadim's offer got my attention, and suddenly my heart and my stomach didn't hurt as much. The idea of returning to Jamaica and seeing Stacy again undermined any sense of loyalty I had left for Yasmine.

"The Canadian authorities are working together with us to take down Ms. Kahn, and they've agreed in principle to grant you immunity in exchange for your cooperation. It's a very generous offer, Cré. You should grab it with both hands. This is the best chance you have to get your life back on track."

He was right about the generosity of the offer, and it seemed to me that either they wanted Yasmine really bad or Nadim had gone out of his way to get me the opportunity of another chance at life.

"I want Bermuda Jack freed and released without charge," I said, trying my best to give the impression that I would sacrifice my future for a man I barely knew.

"That shouldn't be a problem," Nadim replied, barely attempting to conceal a smirk. "Anything else?"

"No," I responded. I wanted to punch Nadim in his handsome face and kiss his smirking lips all at once.

"Good. You'll be staying with me under protective custody while we arraign Ms. Kahn. This is, of course, based on the assumption that you're not going to try to kill me and escape."

Nadim had a twinkle in his eye as if he were expecting me to smile.

"Don't worry. I have nowhere to run to," I replied.

Nadim left the room with me wrestling with feelings of guilt and excitement. Even though I was convinced that Yasmine would kill me on the spot if she saw me, I still had a soft spot for her. But my feelings for her paled in comparison to what I felt for Stacy and the prospect of going home to Jamaica and seeing her.

Two weeks after I was arrested, Yasmine was extradited from Canada to the United States and was charged for the murder of the man she had slashed to death in front of me less than a month before. The man she killed turned out to be an American citizen. A week later, Nadim informed me that Yasmine had requested to see me.

"Why? Is that even allowed?" There was no way I was going to face Yasmine unless it was in a courtroom.

"We worked out a deal with her, and part of the deal is that she gets to talk to you for five minutes."

"Nadim, I don't want to talk to her."

"She's in jail. You're going to be separated by a glass window, and there'll be security guards all around."

"I'm not scared. I just don't want to see her."

"Cré, if you see her today, you may not have to see her in court at all. I need you to do this. It's important."

"Okay. I guess if it's important."

I agreed to see Yasmine mainly out of fear that any lack of cooperation might jeopardize my ticket to freedom. Even though I had signed documentation of my deal, I lived in constant fear that it could be taken away from me at anytime.

Less than two hours later, I was sitting in front of Yasmine. She had dark bags under her eyes, and her oversized, ill-fitting prison garb made her look skinnier than normal. She picked up the phone and indicated with her eyes for me to pick up the phone on my side. I obeyed and put the receiver to my ear, looked away, and braced for the abuse.

"You can look me in the eye. You owe me at least that."

I looked up at Yasmine, and she smiled at me.

"I'm not mad at you, Cré. I can't be. You did what you had to do to survive. I would've done the same thing. Isn't it ironic that I was lecturing you about the dangers of falling in love and now I'm here behind bars because I fell in love with you?"

My eyes opened up wide and focused fully on her face.

"Yes, Cré, I fell head over heels the very first moment I met you. I tried very hard to suppress it, but clearly I lost."

"I'm sorry," I said, averting my eyes again.

"Don't be sorry. You can't help who you love. I'm sure you'll find out how it feels to love someone who doesn't love you back."

"I understand you got a deal," I said, trying to change the uncomfortable topic of our conversation.

"Of course. You think you're the only who knows how to survive? They've agreed to return me to Canada where there's no death penalty."

"How?"

"And this is why I'm amazed you've lasted this long," Yasmine replied with a smirk. "Because I'm not the one they really want. You think the Americans really care that much about some run-of-the-mill drug dealer in Canada? There are way more dangerous people out there in the world."

I looked into Yasmine's condescending stare and wondered how she could be in love with someone who she thought was so naïve.

"Anyway, this is not what I wanted to talk to you about, and I only have five minutes. Your stepfather didn't kill your parents."

"What?" I stopped breathing.

"He ordered their killing, but the triggerman was his brother, Tanny."

"Why are you telling me this, Yasmine?"

"Because I still care about you, believe it or not. I found this out a few months ago, but I didn't want to upset you or have you distracted from your job. I know that you've been pining to go back to Jamaica and resume your old life, but Tanny is still looking for you. I just wanted to warn you so that you can deal with the situation. If you resolve the Tanny situation, then you won't have to run anymore."

27

Whether Yasmine's motives for informing me that Tanny was the triggerman in the shooting of my parents were genuine or not didn't matter. If I wanted to reclaim and resume my old life in Jamaica, I had to get rid of Tanny. The good news was that I had the skills to dispatch Tanny quietly and without any hint of suspicion. I intended to go to Jamaica as soon as I was free to do so, not only to eliminate Tanny but also to make sure my relationship with Stacy was not irreparably damaged. It had increasingly become more important to me to see Stacy again and rekindle the love that, over the time of our separation, I had convinced myself we had. I felt an urgent need to explain to her that I had no choice but to betray the woman in whose care she had left me.

When I informed Nadim that Jamaica was the first place I was going to travel to after my original passport was renewed, he made me aware of a stipulation in the agreement, which I apparently had not read thoroughly, that gave the agency the right to conscript me into its service.

"You're better off staying here and working for the agency than going back to Jamaica and getting in trouble again," he said.

"I need to see Stacy," I pleaded. "I haven't seen or spoken to her in three years."

"That woman is not your friend. She gave you bad advice and left you in the care of one of the most dangerous criminals in North America. I don't think she's the one you should be running to right now, or ever, for that matter. If you go back to Jamaica and get involved with her again, you'll end up dead or in jail. Even though you're free to go back to Jamaica, you can never truly reclaim your life there. You should start a new life here."

I wasn't sure if Nadim was arguing on his own behalf or that of his employer. I cared for Nadim, maybe even loved him, but my hankering for Stacy would not allow me to be his lover, much less commit to him in any way.

"One job and I'm out, right?"

"If that's what you want, Cré."

"What's the job?"

"You're going to the Middle East to take out a Pakistani general. Your handler will give you the details."

"*The Middle East?* Is this the big fish that Yasmine was telling me about? The real one that you guys are after?"

"We've been hearing chatter about al-Qaeda or the Taliban acquiring a nuclear device. Yasmine not only helped us to confirm that the threat is real, she also gave us the identity of the supplier and how to get to him. She actually suggested you for the job to take him out."

"I'm surprised. She doesn't think highly of me." I was convinced now that Yasmine was trying to exact her revenge on me from afar.

"That's not the impression I got in the interrogations. Anyway, in a week's time your handler will brief you. You'll have between now and then to visit your friend. Try to stay out of trouble while you're there."

I was excited at the prospect of returning to Jamaica and seeing Stacy again, but first I planned to take full advantage of the brief window of opportunity I was being granted to take care of Tanny.

The night before I left for Jamaica, I slept in Nadim's bed for the first time since Yasmine had forbidden us to hang out together. Initially, I felt at peace in his arms, as I usually did, but I couldn't stop thinking about Stacy. I became increasingly nervous, anxious, and excited all at the same time.

Early the following morning, I left Nadim asleep in bed and headed straight for the airport.

As the plane touched down at Montego Bay's airport, I pulled out my mirror and stared at my face more out of nervousness than vanity. I wasn't wearing any makeup, and my hair, which I had allowed to grow in the past few weeks but was still short, was dyed light brown like my mother's natural hair color. The nervousness I felt was, I imagined, the same emotion my mother had experienced on our flight back to Jamaica to live permanently. I remembered her reaching for my hand and squeezing it as the plane landed.

I exited the plane and walked across the tarmac toward customs. The combined smells of the ocean and the cooking spices wafting from the airport cafeteria welcomed me home and put the agitated butterflies in my stomach to rest. I picked up my rental car and drove directly to the nearest pharmacy to purchase some of the items I needed for killing Tanny, and then I checked into a hotel close to the airport.

I was at the hotel for less than an hour when the phone rang. It was Stacy. My heart picked up speed, and I stuttered her name in disbelief.

"How did you know I was here?" I asked.

"I need to see you right away. Meet me at the Boscobel airstrip in an hour."

"Oh, okay," I replied nervously.

Stacy hung up without saying anything else. She sounded cold and brusque, and I could only assume that she was not pleased with me. Even so, I still craved to see her. I was certain that her attitude would change once I explained what I had been through.

I jumped into my rented car and headed for Boscobel, which was half an hour away. I intended to get to the airstrip ahead of time so I could survey the location and plot my escape just in case I was being set up. As much as I believed Stacy would do nothing to harm me, I had learned during my time working for Yasmine not to take anything for granted. I couldn't rule out the possibility that Stacy might think I was returning to set her up and that she may try to eliminate me as a threat. I hoped my speculations were just that, not only for the sake of self-preservation but also because Stacy was the only person in Jamaica who could help me to locate Tanny.

The airstrip was quiet with little activity outside except for a landscaper tending to a row of flowering bougainvillea vines separating the parking lot from the runway. Inside the reception area of the hangar was a small family of American tourists and a receptionist. Behind the reception area were two mechanics working on an old single-propeller airplane. I confirmed the arrival time of Stacy's flight and then returned to my car and waited.

Stacy's flight landed fifteen minutes later. From the reception area, I watched her exit the small jet alone. She was dressed in a beige business suit over a white blouse and a pair of pumps the same color as her suit. Her hair was straightened and tied in a ponytail. I couldn't tell her mood, as her countenance was hidden by a pair of aviator shades. Her face seemed rounder than I remembered, and she appeared to have gained some weight. I grew increasingly tense as she approached the reception area.

Once she got inside and saw me, she perched her shades atop her head, flashed a bright warm smile, and approached me with open arms. My body and spirit relaxed and I absorbed her warm embrace. We hugged in silence for a good thirty seconds while I fought back tears.

"Thanks for meeting me on such short notice," Stacy said while she looked me up and down. "You look lean and hard," she continued. "You still running?"

Stacy suggested we find someplace private to talk and asked for my car keys. "Where are we going?" I asked warily as I forfeited the keys.

"There's a secluded beach near Oracabessa. We should have some privacy there," she replied without looking at me.

I shifted in my seat, ran my left hand through my hair, and placed my right arm on the armrest as she sped away from the airstrip. My mind raced trying to come up with an escape plan in case I was heading for an ambush.

In the midst of my fidgeting, Stacy took her eyes off the road for a second, reached for my left hand, and clasped her fingers with mine. She then began talking about our graduating class and what each one was doing with their lives.

After fifteen minutes of our one-way conversation, she pulled off the road, stopping in a patch of red dirt in front of a cluster of sea grape trees that were obscuring the view of the ocean.

I got out of the car and instinctively surveyed my surroundings for any signs that we might have company. I followed Stacy along a narrow path that led through the thicket of grape trees and down to a white-sanded beach no more than a hundred yards wide. I stood and watched her sit on a smooth boulder resting in the shade of the sea grape leaves hanging from the embankment overlooking the beach.

"Cré, come outta the sun and siddown wid mi nuh man," she said while she flipped her shoes off and removed her jacket. "Yuh nuh glad fi si mi?" she continued.

"Stacy, I'm sorry that I testified against Yasmine, but I had no choice," I replied before sitting next to her.

"I should be the one apologizing to you, Cré. I didn't mean to put you in that position. I thought she would have given you some kind of office work, not force you to become her henchman."

"You did the best you could for me at the time. Besides, I could've said no."

"No, you couldn't," Stacy rebutted. "You did what you had to do to survive."

"So you're not angry with me?" I asked sheepishly.

"Is that why yuh suh tense? Yuh think I'm upset wit yuh?"

"The thought did cross my mind. You sounded short over the phone."

"Bitch, if I wanted to do something to you, it woulda happened before you got on the plane. I would never do anything to hurt you." Stacy flashed her bright, white smile and I melted.

My feelings for Stacy, which had taken a backseat to my fears, poked out its timid head. I found myself staring at her full lips and big, warm, brown eyes while I detailed my plans to eliminate Tanny and resume my life in Jamaica and asked for her help finding him. Her smile seemed to dim gradually and then disappear behind a serious countenance when I asked her if she had known that Tanny was the triggerman.

"I didn't find out that he was suspected of being the shooter until after you were sent to the Yukon. Cré, things here are very different from when you left. Tanny took over his brother's business, and it's hard to get to him. He's also looking for you, and if I was able to find out within an hour that you were here and where you were staying, I'm sure he'll find out soon if he hasn't already. I don't have the clout I used to. I had very little in the first place. I'm trying to distance myself from that world anyway. I want to live a normal life. I don't want what happened to my parents to happen to me. I don't want anything to happen to my best friend either."

Stacy paused for a moment. "The best I can do for you right now is help you leave Jamaica ASAP. Today, if you can. I wouldn't even go back to the hotel if I were you. After we're done here, my guy can fly you to Port-au-Prince. You can catch a flight from there back to DC. But before you go, let's take a dip for old times' sake."

I arrived back in Washington, less than twenty-four hours after I had left, lugging a heavy heart and a tangle of emotions. Just hours before, Stacy had convinced me to flee Jamaica, again. But that was not the only source of my angst. She had lured me off the beach into the warm, gentle waves where she surprised me with a hot, passionate kiss that put me in a swoon-fueled daze and made me forget about my double quest to exact revenge against Tanny and remove him from the picture in one stroke.

After a sudden, angry storm cloud burst in a thundering rage and chased us out of the water, Stacy drove us to a nearby villa at Golden Head, and before I knew it, we were making love. It was what I had been dreaming of since we were separated, but for some reason, it felt no different from the times in high school when there was an inebriated victim-to-be blocking our path to true intimacy. Like those times, it felt like she wasn't really into it, like she was putting on an act. I tried desperately to elicit from her the intimate love that I had been yearning for for so long until I realized, frustratingly, that I too was becoming an actor.

At the end of our performance, there was no time for cuddling or conversation, much less an encore. Stacy abruptly closed the curtains on me, rushing me out of the villa, onto her plane, and back on the run into exile in under an hour.

During the hour that it took to fly to Haiti, I endured a wide range of conflicting emotions that left me drained by the time we landed. I wandered around the gloomy, dilapidated airport in Port-au-Prince like a zombie for the two hours I had to wait for the connecting flight to DC. The last thing I recalled thinking before I buried myself in the temporary comfort of the plush, first-class recline was, *What the hell just happened?*

I was revived by the plane bouncing onto the tarmac at RFK International Airport. Minutes later, I stumbled off the plane into the morgue-like fluorescent lighting of the terminal. Travelers and airport staff floated past me like unhappy ghosts as I trudged along the long, lonely trek to the arrivals area, where Nadim had been waiting. The moment I saw his bemused face, feelings of guilt emerged from the troupe of emotions vying for my attention and stood center stage in my thoughts. I tried to mask my emotions with a manufactured smile and infused my gait with forced energy as I approached him.

"Port-au-Prince?" he asked as he accepted my hug.

"Long story," I replied.

"We have time. DC traffic is bad even at one in the morning. You left like a bat outta hell. You didn't even say good-bye."

"I don't want to talk about it right now. Do you mind?"

"Okay. That's fine. As long as you didn't get yourself in any trouble that I have to clean up." Nadim smiled at me nervously.

"No trouble," I muttered as I ran my hands through my hair.

"No baggage, huh?"

"Just me," I replied.

Nadim hugged me and this time drew me into him, as if he understood everything I was feeling and was trying to comfort me. I felt forgiven in his embrace. Even though we had never consummated our relationship, I felt that I had betrayed him by hankering for Stacy and inevitably sleeping with her.

I held on to his arm as he led me on a straight path through the lively traffic of bodies milling around in the arrivals area, past the bustling traffic in the pick-up area, and into the clear, cloudless night.

I had never missed Nadim more than I missed him now. I regretted never making love to him. It was understood that it would not be wise for us to be intimately involved while Yasmine's case was being decided. I suppose he also wanted to avoid being a distraction that might jeopardize the success of my mission. I wished that I hadn't been so hung up over Stacy and that I had been more aggressive with him, especially now that I was staring evil in the eye and for the first time was worried that I may not make it back to Nadim alive. This evil gave no name and declared no rank, but I saw in his steady, gray gaze and his humorless smile that he was in charge.

So far, everything had gone as planned. I was among a dozen girls who had responded to an online ad seeking American models for a music video to be shot in Abu Dhabi. We were all arrested at the airport for bringing drugs into the Emirates and bailed out two hours later by a man that looked and sounded like Borat. He was dressed in a white suit and white-framed sunglasses and introduced himself as "the producer."

The girls, some that looked as young as fifteen, pleaded their innocence but were given the choice of "working off" the cost of their bail or going back to jail where they might be raped or worse. The girls all looked at me after they were presented with the frightful options—I had become the girls' de facto leader, as I was the most vociferous and articulate when we got arrested.

At that moment, I remembered my handler at the agency instructing me over and over that this was not a mission to save victims of sex trafficking but to kill General Aziz. But I couldn't help but try to protect the girls who looked to me with frightened faces, so I railed at the false choice we were being given.

The producer lifted his sunglasses, looked at me, and then nodded in my direction, after which two burly, tanned men approached me with intent. I kicked one in the groin and punched the other in the throat before I felt the cold barrel of a gun jammed against the side of my head. The girls screamed, and the producer ordered them to shut up before grabbing me by the hair and sliding the point of his gun around to the middle of my forehead. Two more men appeared and he ordered them to take me out of the room.

"Don't worry, guys. Everything's gonna be okay," I lied as I was carted away.

Now I was sitting in front of the real "producer" and feared that my cover was blown. I watched him nervously as he leafed through my passport.

"Pepper Parker," he read before resuming his stare. "Your parents knew you'd be a feisty one, didn't they. Based on what I've observed so far, you're multilingual and seem well traveled, yet your passport is blank."

"I recently renewed it," I replied.

"You're different from the other girls. Perhaps we can help each other. You seem to want to help the other girls, and I need a smart, beautiful fighter. I have a client who would pay very well to spend an evening with a girl with your special qualities. This would go a long way to paying down the debt of you and your friends."

I understood what he was proposing, and I was relieved that my cover was not blown. But I also knew that the girls would be forced into prostitution within the next twenty-four hours and there was nothing I could do about it. I asked for specifics, and he promised that the girls would work as strippers only but would also be offered the opportunity to "make more money" only if they wanted to.

He also promised that the girls would be safe unless they attempted to run.

I was punished with the painful task of informing the other girls that they would have to work as strippers until their bail was paid off and that they had the option of working off their obligations faster if they also worked as prostitutes. I looked each girl in the eye as I broke the terrible news, hoping to communicate strength and a sense of belief that we would survive this ordeal together. But I was a wreck on the inside.

I was heartbroken and wracked with guilt as I helplessly watched the girls trafficked out at nighttime, each leaving with her head held low and returning the next morning with her head hanging even lower. I tried to play comforter, but a well of resentment toward me had formed because they couldn't help but notice that I was neither stripping nor turning tricks. I couldn't tell them that I actually got the shittier end of the deal, that I was being saved for a client who had killed or maimed every girl that was sold to him.

Things came to a head four days into the ordeal when one of the girls indirectly accused me of being in on the whole thing. I was increasingly isolated and kept to myself for the next few days, until I was put in the care of a woman dressed in a black chador that covered everything except for a pair of big, smoldering, brown eyes.

The woman cut my hair and styled it conservatively like that of a politician's wife. She dressed me in a dark blue pair of pants and a white blouse under a red blazer with an American flag pin attached to the left lapel. I was also given a pair of two-inch, block-heeled red pumps to wear with my conservative outfit. The final item was a narrow belt that she meticulously threaded through each loop around my waist. At that moment, I knew that she was the "man" we had on the inside.

With the murder weapon securely fastened around my waist, I was led to the office of the man who had heartlessly conscripted so many girls into sexual slavery and who had handpicked me as my target's next victim.

He looked me up and down before ordering me to sit. "If you want to return alive and in one piece, you must do exactly as I say. The last nine girls didn't completely follow my instructions, and they didn't make it back."

"How many were there before me?" I asked.

"Nine," he responded nonchalantly before continuing. "My client wants a feisty American woman with no fear in her eyes. He is going to order you to get naked, but you must refuse. He will then attack you and force himself on you, and it's important that you resist with all of your might. When he has conquered you and is having his way with you, make sure you cry loudly and tears are streaming from your eyes."

I was warned by my handler that I might be drugged and possibly sexually assaulted, but that conversation didn't quite prepare me for how casually I was being readied for violent assault and rape. I had not been afraid up to this point, and I hoped my changing countenance did not reveal the trepidation I was experiencing. I wondered why Nadim didn't do more to ensure that I wasn't given such a dangerous assignment. I started to question whether he truly loved me or was using me.

The sociopath with the dead eyes and cold smile continued to throw instructions at me as matter-of-factly as a director prepping an actor for a role. I could feel my quiet fear transforming to a raging anger barely being kept in check by the memory of my handler's oft-repeated directive: "General Aziz is the target, not the sexual trafficker. You're not going there to save the girls." I felt like killing the monster sitting in front of me and fleeing, but it was too late to run.

I was driven to an oasis somewhere in the middle of the desert, where I was handed over to two tall, burly, mustachioed men. The men who had driven here immediately drove off in the direction from which we came. This confirmed in my mind that I was not expected to survive and my body was slated to be buried somewhere in the anonymous expanse of sand just behind this dusty town.

I instinctively surveyed my surroundings, mapping out possible escape routes. Even though I was assured that I would be tracked and an escape plan had been prearranged, I didn't want to take any chances. There was a fleet of black SUVs with tinted windows idling in front of a small, two-story motel. There were a half dozen discretely armed men smoking, chatting, and laughing.

I was escorted into the motel, past a vacant reception area, and up a flight of stairs toward a room in the center of the second floor.

I was ushered into the room where General Aziz was lounging in a chaise, thumbing away on a BlackBerry. He was dressed in full army regalia—khaki uniform with bulky epaulettes, shiny medals, and knee-high, shiny, black boots. He was also wearing a black holster with the ivory butt of a pistol pointing toward me. On a lamp table beside him was a pair of gold-rimmed aviator shades and a peaked general's cap.

He grunted an order to the men who then left and closed the door behind them. He continued to type away on his device and did not turn his head in my direction. I remained standing in the same spot where the men had left me, waiting for Aziz to make the first move.

"Take your clothes off and get on the bed," he mumbled, without looking away from his BlackBerry.

"Excuse me?" I snapped back with as much American accented incredulity as I could conjure. "Look, buddy, I don't know what you think this is, but I was told that the only thing I'd be doing is attending some kinda function with you as your date, nothing more. So if you're looking for something else, you can forget about it." I walked toward him as I retorted, partly to give him the impression that I wasn't afraid but mostly to see, through the window behind him, what was at the back of the hotel. There was only one SUV there with one man leaning against it smoking a cigarette.

My visualization of escape abruptly ended when Aziz sprang from his chair and slapped me across the face so hard I thought my eyes would pop out of their sockets. I screamed and fell backward onto the king-size bed. He marched at me and then grabbed me by the throat.

"Madame Secretary, this is not the White House, and you're not Obama's bitch anymore. You're mine. Take your clothes off now, whore!" He released his vicelike grip on my throat and began to strip off his uniform. He stopped undressing with his pants and boots still on and pulled a riding crop from his boots before removing his gun from its holster.

"I'm not scared of you," I lied as I jumped from my sitting position to a kneeling stance on the bed. I stared at him defiantly while my heart pounded away, hoping that he wouldn't shoot me.

"Boris was right about you," he said as he grinned and placed the gun on the lamp table beside him. "I'm going to enjoy this."

He approached me slowly and deliberately, like a hunter stalking its prey. He twirled his moustache with his free hand and slapped the riding crop against his thigh with each step toward the bed.

I backed away cautiously, crouching on all fours like a cornered wild animal, ready to pounce or run.

I had been warned that, in his youth, General Aziz was an accomplished wrestler and a highly trained hand-to-hand combat fighter, so I was concerned that the defensive wrestling stance I had assumed—legs wide and torso forward—might tip him off to the fact that I was not one of his usual victims. But he seemed too turned on by the challenge to notice. I didn't want to give him enough time to realize that I knew what I was doing and might actually be dangerous, so I allowed him to corner me, upon which he took the opportunity to swing his riding crop at me. I dodged the blow and made sure I fell onto the bed on my back. He then grabbed my left leg and began to thrash me with the riding crop.

There was hatred and bloodlust in Aziz's wide, black, excited eyes, and he transformed into the dark, faceless monster from my nightmares. The monster got more and more excited as I engaged in a choreographed orgy of screaming, writhing, and flailing. It seemed to grow in stature and menace, arrogantly tossing aside the riding crop, grabbing me by the throat, and attempting to mount me.

This presented me with the opening I was waiting for, which I ruthlessly exploited with a swift, firm kick between its haunches.

Time stood still as I raced to take advantage of the split-second window that the monster's temporary debilitation allowed me. Before it could fully collapse on top of me, I slipped from underneath it, jumped on its back, and pulled the murder weapon from my belt in one smooth action. I wrapped the high-tensile polymer wire around the monster's neck and pulled tight. I then flipped on my back and locked my legs around its torso to prevent its escape. While I pulled with all my might, I screamed and begged and groaned for the benefit of the audience just outside the door.

As the monster heaved and struggled to escape, I was aroused at the sight of the ring of blood forming around its neck and the sensation and sounds of its gasping, futilely grappling final throes.

While I continued to make moaning and crying sounds, I checked to make sure the monster had no more pulse, and then I jammed the room door handle with a chair before twining a rope from the sheets to lower myself from the window.

Outside the window, there was no guard in sight, although the SUV was still there. I took the general's gun along with his cap and aviator shades and lowered myself with one hand while the other hand alternately aimed the gun at the exit to the rear of the motel and the SUV just in case the guard returned or emerged from the SUV and tried to shoot me. My left hand burned from the friction caused by my swift descent, and my knees hurt from my hard landing. I made a limping, crouching dash for the SUV with the dead general's gun firmly in my grip and aiming forward.

Less than fifteen feet from the idling SUV, the passenger door shot open.

"Get in. Hurry up," an American-accented voice urged.

I rushed into the SUV, and it sped off with me before I could even close the door, which slammed shut from the momentum of the vehicle lurching forward.

The driver, who had a similar mop hairstyle and moustache, and who was wearing sunglasses identical to that worn by the guard standing next to the SUV, crashed the vehicle through a wooden gate leading into the desert, leaving a billowing cloud of dust and sand in its wake. Laid out in the backseat with a bullet hole in his head was the missing guard.

About a half minute after driving at top speed, I saw a fleet of SUVs coming after us. Three tense minutes later, we arrived at a waiting helicopter. The driver and I scampered into the helicopter, which quickly whisked us away to safety.

Within the next twenty-four hours, I was debriefed; relieved of General Aziz's gun, cap, and aviator shades; and put on a plane back to Washington, DC. During the debriefing, I was informed that the girls with whom I was abducted were rescued shortly after Aziz's death was verified and that most of the traffickers were in the custody of the Abu Dhabi police.

I leapt into Nadim's arms the moment he opened the door after arriving at his home from the airport. We kissed as if we hadn't seen each other in years. All the repressed and unexpressed feelings that I had for him, which I feared would die with me during the most dangerous moments of my mission, surged from my body, and we attacked each other in a furious bout of lovemaking. It was the best sex I had ever had, and I was convinced it was love until he spoke.

"That was outstanding," he said while catching his breath. He was lying on his back in bed beside me and staring at the ceiling.

I thought he was talking about our lovemaking, so I cuddled up closer to him and kissed his sweat-soaked cheek. I had one arm lying across his hairy, heaving chest and one leg loped across his thighs. I stared at the sweat streaming down the side of his handsome face.

"You should continue working with the agency," he continued.

I sighed, slid my arm and leg off his body, and turned my back to him.

"It's just a suggestion, Cré. You're not obligated to do anything more for the agency. But it would be nice to put your special skills to good use for them, especially in light of how generous they've been with you."

I did not respond, and he said nothing more.

Over the next couple of minutes, his heavy breathing gradually subsided to the steady whispers of sleep. I slid out of bed and went straight into the shower.

As I stood underneath the shower, I wondered if Nadim really loved me or if I was being typically naïve.

How could a man talk about work right after finally consummating a relationship three years in the making? If he loved me, why would he encourage me to continue this line of work? Did he not care that I could have been brutally raped or killed? Has he just been using me all along?

Doubts about Nadim's true feelings for me streamed out of my mind and allowed space for my infatuation with Stacy to seep into. Slowly but surely, I fell prey to the notion that Stacy was my only true hope for happiness. But Tanny's presence in Jamaica stood as a barrier between Stacy and me.

After showering, I went back to bed determined to renew my effort to take out Tanny and resume my life with Stacy.

Early the next morning, I packed and snuck out while Nadim was still sleeping. I took a taxi to the airport and booked the earliest flight to Bogota, Colombia, where I hoped to reacquaint myself with my former, and favorite, stepfather, Sebastien. My mother hadn't kept in touch with any of my stepfathers, and she hadn't allowed me to. With the exception of my biological father, it was always a clean break. But I was visiting Sebastien not only to catch up with him but also to seek his help with dispatching Tanny.

My flight left at 7:00 a.m. and arrived in Bogota around 12:30 p.m. local time. When I showed up unannounced at Sebastien's home in an upscale enclave on the outskirts of Bogota, he was gleefully surprised. He seemed shorter and heavier than when I last had seen him, and he had gray streaks in his thick, salon-styled hair, but his smile was just as warm as I remembered it. He had not remarried but was in the company of a beautiful, tall, bespectacled brunette whom he introduced as his lawyer. She was dressed in a navy-blue business suit whose hem seemed a bit short for business. The woman, who eyed me suspiciously, excused herself, and Sebastien and I spent the next few hours reminiscing about my mother and our too brief time as a family.

Sebastien had held on to a romanticized memory of my mother. He credited her with changing his life for the better, after she divorced him upon discovering he was a drug trafficker. According to him, she inspired him to clean up his act and convert his drug-fueled wealth into legitimate businesses. He seemed convinced that had he changed fast enough or tried harder to keep her, she would still be alive and still in his arms.

I tried to leverage the strong affection he still had for her to get the help I needed to exact revenge on her killer.

"I have some old friends that owe me some favors," he replied.

Within two days, he had arranged to sneak me into Jamaica with the intelligence and the supplies I requested. A day later, as we were saying our good-byes, he asked me if I was sure killing Tanny would be the right thing to do.

"I'm sure," I replied without hesitation.

"After your mother left me and I decided to change my life, one of the hardest decisions I had to make was not killing one of my rivals who had killed my favorite nephew. I had to sacrifice my desire for revenge so that I could have a real chance to leave the old life behind. It was hard, but that was the price I had to pay. Nothing in life is free, especially happiness and peace of mind."

He ran his fingers through my hair and rearranged a couple of strands as he smiled.

I had a flashback to when Sebastien used to braid my hair before dropping me off at grade school. My mother would watch us with a mixture of bemusement and happiness.

She had a different reaction though when she discovered that he had taught me to shoot and gave me target practice sessions each day after school. The lessons came in handy one night when an intruder broke in and tried to kill Sebastien. I shot the would-be assassin in the head twice with one of Sebastien's many guns littered throughout our home. That night proved to be the death knell of my mother's marriage to Sebastien, which ended a month later. I was only ten years old and, for a long time afterward, blamed myself for ruining my mother's marriage.

I thanked Sebastien and then hugged and kissed him good-bye before leaving in a waiting taxi. As the cab drove off, I looked back to see Sebastien waving good-bye. And just like when my mother left with me more than a decade ago, tears welled in my eyes and ran down my face.

Under the cover of night, I was flown from a remote airstrip outside Bogota to another remote airstrip near the southwestern coast of Haiti. From Haiti, I took a boat that dropped me off at the easternmost tip of Jamaica. By the time it took me to hike the two miles from the port to the private villa where I would be based while I carried out my new mission, it was already dawn. I went straight to bed and slept until the monster from dreams past returned and woke me four hours later. I had only a two-and-a-half-day window in which to kill Tanny and return to the rendezvous point to be transported back to Colombia, so I got out of bed and went over my plan.

It was Wednesday, and I was to be picked up at dusk on Friday.

According to the intelligence that Sebastien provided me, every other Thursday Tanny visited a small, rural district in the Blue Mountain region of the Parish of Portland, where he owned a coffee plantation. At the end of the day, he hung out at a local bar with some of his employees who worked on the plantation and then spent the night at a house he owned in the area before returning to his main residence in Kingston the next day. My plan was to get into his Blue Mountain retreat after his night of drinking and make his death look like an accident.

I hopped on one of the two lime-green Kawasaki dirt bikes available for use at the villa and rode thirty miles of mountain roads to case out Tanny's house, the bar, and the route between the bar and his house. The one-hour drive took me along winding roads bordered by lush vegetation and steep inclines and declines with spectacular mountain views. At times, I caught myself fantasizing about hiking the mountain trails with Stacy.

Tanny's cottage was conspicuously enclosed by nine-foot, limestone-white walls topped by broken glass. All the other nearby houses were bordered by deteriorating wood and barbed-wire fences, if at all. The entrance was secured by wrought-iron gates, and the property had complete perimeter camera coverage. Two German shepherds stalked the grounds in between bouts of play fighting. About two miles from Tanny's cottage was the local bar, a wooden shack with a corrugated zinc roof.

By the end of the day, I had devised a plan and a few contingencies.

The following day, I woke up at 10:00 a.m. after sleeping for twelve hours. I had used some of the sleeping agent I had planned to use on Tanny to help me bypass the monster from my nightmares. Then I spent the rest of the daylight hours going over my plan, making sure I had all my tools ready and functioning properly.

By nightfall, I was in Tanny's district and had hidden my dirt bike in a thicket of bush a quarter mile from the bar. I walked to the bar where a number of vehicles were parked on a patch of dirt at the rear. There was no lighting where the vehicles were parked, and after making sure no one was loitering outside the bar, I snuck into Tanny's unlocked vehicle, an old Toyota 4Runner, and lay down on the floor between the third- and second-row seats.

Two hours later, around midnight, I heard laughter before the front passenger door opened. I had my hand in my knapsack with my finger on the trigger of my gun just in case. Someone sat in the front passenger seat, after which the door was closed. The driver's door opened a few seconds after.

"Tanny, yuh sure yuh can drive?" a woman's voice asked with a slur. "Yuh drunk as skunk."

"Yuh wah drive?" Tanny replied.

"A dead yuh wah dead? Yuh no si seh mi more mash up dah yuh?"

"Aaright den. Jus sekkle yuhself an mek the liquor drive we home," Tanny declared before shutting the door.

I began to prepare mentally for a double killing.

"Yuh smell dat?" the woman asked as Tanny drove off.

"Smell wah?" Tanny replied.

"Yuh cyar smell like white woman. Tanny, yuh a hypocrite yuh know? How come every time mi invite yuh over yuh chat bout yuh love yuh wife but yuh a fuck white woman inna yuh cyar?"

"No, man. A cedar tree yuh a smell."

"Tanny, yuh tink mi a fool? Mi know di difference between white woman smell an cedar tree smell."

"Mi swear pon mi likkle son head mi nah cheat pon mi wife wid nobody, Patricia."

"Aaright. Calm down. But yuh car still smell like white woman."

An eternal moment of silence passed in which I literally held my breath, hoping that the woman's suspicions didn't lead to my discovery.

"Yuh know Tanny, mi rememba when yuh used to call mi Trish. Now yuh married to dis hoity-toity town girl an all of a sudden yuh a call mi Patricia. Mi glad say yuh outta de drugs business an yuh a try do good things wid yuh life, but yuh haffi rememba seh mi nevah judge yuh when yuh was living the bad man life. Mi know seh me is jus a likkle country girl, but yuh likkle rich wife can neva love yuh as much as me love yuh. A bet yuh she cyan even cook. Anyway, a suh life go. The one them wah yuh love always love somebody else."

The SUV slowed to a stop, and I heard both doors open and close. The passengers stepped out. I exhaled a huge sigh of relief.

"You don' have to walk me to ma door. I'm aright. I'm sorry 'bout what a said. I'm happy dat yuh happy."

"See yuh in two weeks," Tanny said.

I heard a gate creak open and then shut and then a door opening and slamming shut. Tanny returned to the SUV and drove off.

"Don't move, motherfucker, and don't make a sound," I said quietly but firmly. I had the silencer tip of my gun planted firmly in the nape of Tanny's neck. "Put your hands behind the seat."

Tanny complied, glancing in the rearview mirror as he pulled his hand away from the garage-door remote.

"Whose truck is that? Who else is here?" I asked as I bound his hands behind his seat with a plastic tie. There was a red BMW X7 SUV parked in the second garage space next to us.

"Das mine," Tanny responded quietly and calmly. "Das wha mi drive from town. Nobody else nuh de yah. Mi always leave de 4Runner here. Mi nuh have no money inna de house, but yuh can tek de Beama."

I used another plastic tie to bind Tanny's neck to the metal spindles holding up his headrest. I took the garage remote from the visor and took a pair of tranquilizer guns out of my knapsack. I got out of the car and shot the two German shepherds, which were loitering just outside the garage door. I immediately pressed the remote to close the garage door, and both dogs yelped and growled before making a futile dash to get at me. But the door shut.

I turned my attention back to Tanny, who had somehow dislodged his left shoe and was attempting to retrieve a box cutter from the glove compartment of the truck with his toes. I pressed one of the tranquilizer guns against his neck, and he pulled back his foot.

I returned the tranquilizer guns to the knapsack, which was lying on the passenger seat behind Tanny. I retrieved my gun and took out a syringe and a small, clear glass bottle that contained the sleeping agent I intended to use on Tanny. I then faced Tanny and pointed my gun at his forehead, before pulling off the black baseball cap I was wearing.

"Cré?" he said calmly, almost in a whisper.

"How does it feel to be the one looking down the barrel of a gun?" I seethed. "You're going to pay for what you did to my parents."

"A was jus doin ma job. I was a different person then. I didn't know any betta. Mi sorry."

"'Sorry' ain't gonna cut it," I said as I tucked my gun in my waist. I then began to draw the sleeping agent from its bottle by using the syringe.

Tanny squirmed in his seat, and his eyes bulged in a panic. "Please, don't do dis. A have a likkle son. Him only one an' a half." Even though his countenance was screaming panic, his voice was low, as if he didn't want the walls to know he was scared.

"Why should I show you any mercy? You didn't show my mother any mercy, and she had a child."

"I coulda kill yuh when yuh wuz in Mobay two months ago, but I didn't."

"Liar. You missed your opportunity because I left before you could get to me."

"No, no. Is because a decide to change ma life. I'm a farmer and a happy family man now. You can be happy too if yuh jus spare my life and walk away from the killin' business."

"Don't you dare compare us. We're not the same. I killed your brother in self-defense, but you killed my parents out of spite."

"Yuh just like how I used to be. Mi know seh yuh used fi dun up people fi Yasmine."

"Listen, mister, you should be thanking me that I decided not to take out your wife and kid. Now stop talking before I change my mind. Open your mouth."

Tanny meekly complied. He seemed to have accepted the inevitability of his fate.

I jammed the syringe in his mouth and squirted the sleeping agent down his throat. He involuntarily swallowed and then coughed.

"Promise mi yuh won' harm mi wife an son no matta what. Please, mi a beg yuh."

"Sure," I replied.

"No. Seh yuh promise . . . du . . . mi a beg yuh."

"Okay, I promise. Now stop talking."

"Tanks," he slurred as he faded into unconsciousness.

I quickly deposited the syringe and the empty drug container into my knapsack and then removed the plastic ties from around Tanny's hands and neck. I started the SUV and rolled down all the windows. I then tripped the circuit breaker, which was located on the wall facing the front of the SUVs, and donned my night-vision goggles before exiting through the garage's side door. I walked around to the front of the garage and pulled the tranquilizer darts from the unconscious dogs. I then scaled the front gate and ran the one and three-quarter miles to the location where I had hidden my dirt bike.

It was cold and misty on the lonely ride back to the villa. The mountain roads, so full of life and spectacular views during daytime, now felt treacherous. I drove at lower than normal speeds and with the carefulness that poor visibility dictated, but I was constantly worried about plunging off the road. At times, it felt like vertigo, like I was being pulled by some dark force over the edge down toward the scary, dark valley below.

I thought I would be happy, but I wasn't. I was on a speedboat heading to Haiti and silently watching the evening fade into the inevitable night. I hadn't slept the night before after returning from Tanny's house, not because of the monster from my nightmares but because I couldn't get Tanny out of my mind. He seemed not to be the monster I had imagined he was. I tried to take my mind off Tanny by visualizing my future with Stacy, but my fantasies eventually faded and were replaced by memories of his face. Like twilight being overtaken by darkness.

When I got back to Bogota early Saturday morning, I booked into a hotel and slept all day with the help of sleeping pills. On Sunday morning, I called Sebastien to inform him of my success and to thank him for his help. He was his excited self when I initially called, but at the end of our brief conversation, he was less ebullient and seemed disappointed. I knew he was hoping I had had a change of heart about killing Tanny, but I didn't think he understood that it was the only way to get my life back.

Immediately after I got off the phone, I booked the next flight to DC. I owed it to Nadim to let him know I would be returning to Jamaica permanently. I landed in DC in the evening and arrived at Nadim's home just before sunset.

Before I even had a chance to put down my luggage, Nadim gave me a tight, long embrace.

"I'm so glad you're back. I didn't think I'd ever see you again. You left without saying anything."

"Sorry about that. I went to Colombia to clear my head."

"I'm sorry. I'm not very good at this romance thing, but I should have said this from the very outset: I love you. I'm a little slow, but I realized, after you left, that I was a jerk for yapping about work right after sharing one of the best moments of my life with you. You make me happy, Cré, and I want to make you happy too."

I hadn't planned for this. I didn't know what to say. "Can I have a drink?"

"Sure." Nadim took my luggage and headed for his bedroom. "What do you want?"

"Whiskey, straight." I sat down on the edge of the couch and stared at the glass coffee table in front of me.

"One whiskey coming up," Nadim said as he returned from the bedroom. I think I'll have one too to celebrate us."

"Nadim, I have to talk to you about something."

"Cré, I know this is a lot to put on you right now, but I just wanted you to know unequivocally how I felt about you. Now that you're back we can talk—" His cell phone vibrated, rattling loudly on the glass table. He handed me the glass of whiskey and picked up the phone. "What's up?" he said to the caller.

I practically downed the entire glass of whiskey while trying to come up with the best way to tell Nadim that I intended on returning to Jamaica and therefore couldn't be with him. I was focused so much on what I was going to say that I didn't even realize that Nadim had disappeared out of the room, until I noticed him walking back out of the bedroom.

"Cré . . ."

"Nadim, I have to tell you something," I blurted. I was still holding the empty whiskey glass.

"I know, honey, but I just found out something that you should know right now." Nadim sat beside me and took the whiskey glass from me and held my hands. The way he was looking at me began to concern me.

"What?"

"Your friend in Jamaica, Stacy, died a couple days ago. I'm sorry."

It took a few moments for what he said to register before I pulled my hands out of his hands, shoved him away from me, and got up from the couch.

"Apparently, her husband got home drunk and passed out at the wheel before turning off his car. She and her husband and their baby died of carbon monoxide poisoning."

"Stacy isn't married. She doesn't have a baby."

"She had been married for almost two years. She and her husband had a year-and-a-half-old son."

"Liar! You're just trying to stop me from going back home! You're a fucking liar!"

"I'm truly sorry, Cré." Nadim walked slowly toward me with his arms wide open.

"Stay away from me!" I backed into the wall behind me.

The room began to spin and the monster from my nightmares seeped out of the walls like a black mist, sucked the breath from my mouth, and consumed all the light.

About the Author

Dean Campbell was born in Jamaica and migrated to the United States to attend college. Even though he incurred a small mortgage while earning a bachelor's degree in economics and mathematics at Columbia University, writing is his passion, third only to his twin loves of soccer and Scrabble. He is the author of *Eboné Blue* (2006) and currently works and resides in New York City.